I0575673

AROUND

THOMAS MCFADDEN

Published by Czar House Studios

ISBN: 979-8-9998105-0-2 (ebook) | 979-8-9998105-2-6 (paperback) | 979-8-9998105-3-3 (hardcover) | 979-8-9998105-1-9 (audiobook)

This is a work of fiction. The story, all names, characters, businesses, places, events, and incidents portrayed in this production are fictitious and are a product of the author's imagination. Any identification, resemblance, or references to real people (living or deceased), real events, or historical events is unintended, should not be inferred, and is entirely coincidental.

Paperback cover design by Anze Ban Virant - ABV atelier design

Hardback cover design by Aaron Grant

First edition. | October 2025.

After finishing this book, please head over to https://www.aroundth enovel.com/game to play the novel's immersive game experience on the AppStore, Android, and PC.

AROUND – The Game

After finishing the novel, return to this page to play AROUND - The Game—an immersive and terrifying, first-person experience inside the world of the novel. You can download and play the game on the App Store, Android, or PC by going to https://www.aroundthenovel.com/game or by scanning the QR code below with your smartphone or tablet.

Innocence is dead.

AROUND

1

Wrought iron skewered the pale sky. The spear-tipped finials dug into the calmness of the day. Nate studied their pointed thrust with undue admiration. Had his friends known what he was hiding—what they all were hiding—they'd have thought twice about coming here.

Even with the oppressive humidity, no day had been better than this to find what they were searching for. They stood before the tall, black gate with necks arched and eyes squinting at the fervent sun, its sharp rays dousing them in the safety of daylight.

"Everyone remember the rules?" said Ruth, who was tying back her dense, blonde hair in a knot. Her flaxen mane glowed like bars of gold and was practically as heavy. Underneath the bars, her sapphire eyes shone just as excitedly.

"It's hard to forget something you've been told a dozen times," said Amir. He loved to challenge Ruth's self-proclaimed authority, or any authority, for that matter.

"Rule Number 1: The house does not like visitors. Once you find the house, you can only go back to it within that same day. Once that day ends, if you so much as look at the house, you'll die. So, you better take this in because it's the last time you'll ever see it." She was referring to the gate and the haunting splendor that lay beyond.

"Too bad," said Olivia, looking like she was going to be sick. The nervous sarcasm in her voice wasn't an unusual device in her coping arsenal, but here, her frown was practically sewn on as she surveyed the malevolent iron spires.

"It's really something," said Daphne evenly. Her efforts to hide her excitement for the experience only made her more conspicuous. As if to confirm this, she jerked to scratch her arm and gnashed her bottom lip.

The house was visible about three hundred feet past the gate. It was massive and stone—a fortress of craftsmanship. The home's ornate architecture contrasted with its decay, which, if the theories about its age were true, was nowhere near as prevalent as it should've been. Gilded beauty still teased from under viny overgrowth.

"Rule Number 2," Ruth continued, "If you find *the dark*, you can never find it again. Rule Number 3: If you are in *the dark* after the sun sets, you can never—EVER—leave it."

"Ever," Amir repeated with a mocking smile.

"And finally, Rule Number 4: If you are still inside the house after the sun sets, not only will you never find your way out, but the demon will be let out of *the dark*."

"I'm just going in to know if I'll make it out." Amir's classic smirk persisted, as though the edges of his mouth were stapled to his upper cheeks.

"With your track record, Amir, we won't be counting on it. Sunset's at 8:43. Which means we're out of there by 8:15 at the latest. Got it?"

They all "got it," but none were exactly sure what there was to get. It was somewhat of a joke, especially to Nate, who could hardly even remember agreeing to come all the way out here. He supposed it was his passive nature, merely taking charge without his permission, the same way a madman kills and then moseys on down to a coffee shop to enjoy a latte or iced matcha, having no recollection of his heinous crime.

Their early start had given them an opportunity for maximum daylight at the house and *the dark*, if they could find it, but they'd wasted hours in the woods going in circles before finally winding upon the great gate.

They were there for one reason only: to find *the dark*. No one knew if it actually existed. It was one of those down-the-line rumors. Ruth heard about it from someone who heard about it from someone else and so on. It was different than a legend or a myth. It wasn't like everyone in town knew about it, and your grandparents had been when they were kids. No, it wasn't that. It was a rumor that never quite gained mainstream traction but always managed to hang around.

The dark was some sort of space beyond time and consciousness. It was a place to access the deeper parts of the mind, or so everyone said. Apparently, once inside, one could speak to a dark entity, some kind of demon. This demon was a digger who could shovel through the thick of your thoughts and determine if any jewels lay hidden in the mire. Nate, though he still couldn't remember how he'd wound up here, couldn't forget that part, which Ruth had mentioned the other day. He couldn't fathom why on earth anyone would want to converse with such evil forces, himself being a person of faith. However, underneath all that suppression was something he couldn't quite pinpoint, and wasn't sure he wanted to, but it possessed the slightest taste of curiosity. If anything, he supposed he wanted to know who he was going to be, to know his higher purpose, and seeing as God had yet to show him, perhaps this demon or whatever it was could instead. But there was something else inside Nate. Something the others didn't see. And the way he studied those sharp finials and their hostile shape, there was a twistedness in his gaze, revealing that he knew exactly why he'd come here.

The gate swung inward with surprising ease. Its dry iron *eeeeeeked* on the hinges. The sound was piercing and skin-crawling, like the sound of a rat caught in a grate slowly becoming further wedged with each squirm for release. All five kids shuddered and clenched at the noise. Olivia nearly smacked her glasses into the gravel. Nonetheless, were it not for the awful creak, she probably would've found a way to do that anyway. She had a clumsiness to her that was almost charming. It was a paradox. Her failure to recognize that she had any sort of pretty quality, let alone her terrible awkwardness, made her that much more endearing.

Making their way into the courtyard, the house sneered down at them. Was it four stories? Was it five? Six? It was hard to tell. The unevenness of the architecture was intimidating and appeared to lean forward as if held up by wires, like it could fall on them at any moment.

Wicked-faced gargoyles and steepled chimneys stabbed into the swollen air. The home had an energy to it, a dark energy. In the same way that a confident person exudes charisma, the house emitted hate. You couldn't see it like you could the pollen coating the limestone exterior, but you could feel it.

Olivia ran her hand along the degraded curvature of the fountain. The weathered marble had hardly grayed or etched with time, like it should have. The stone was unexpectedly smooth under her soft skin. She pushed the pollen back into golden clumps and sneezed, her glasses nearly flying off again. Readjusting the wire rims, she took a closer look. To her surprise, under the yellow dust, the marble retained its shine.

"It should be matte," Olivia said, more to herself.

What was stranger was that the home had no clear main entrance, only some elongated windows that wouldn't budge despite Ruth's persistence.

"Nobody said we wouldn't be able to get in," said Amir.

"Nobody said we'd get this far, either," Ruth scoffed. "Nobody would know about the dark if they'd never gotten in."

"So…," Daphne murmured with an impatient flutter of her fingers.

"So, let's swing around the side."

As they did just that, something caught Nate's attention. It was a dormer perched on the roof, jutting out from the main slope—an attic window, maybe. Iron casing formed a cross on the outside of the pane, perfectly square and roughly four feet by four feet, sitting alone on that section of the roof. It beckoned to Nate, and the curiosity that he was relentlessly suppressing became a little less opaque.

There was nothing on the side of the home but eight feet of limestone below windows that didn't seem to open or close.

Statues of the Baroque and Neoclassical vein littered the home's larger, rear courtyard with its maze of symmetrical walking paths. The statues similarly seemed to have avoided corrosion. Other than the pollen robes that dressed them, the sculptures appeared pristine and purified.

Nate looked at Ruth. "Who lived here?"

"Nobody."

"No one would build something like this just to forget about it."

"I thought you had met my parents," Amir said with his patented grin.

Ruth rolled her eyes. "The house isn't a home, though it may look like one. It's just a structure. It wasn't built. It just exists. No one lives here. No one ever has. No one ever will."

"Is that just because they couldn't get in?" said Olivia. She could be funny when she wanted to, and she wanted to, usually, more than her friends would like.

Nate ignored her. "So, it just appeared then? From nothing?"

"You don't trust me. Do you, Nate?"

"It's not like you've given me any reasons not to."

Ruth laughed and bit her bottom lip in such a manner that she hoped only Nate would see, but Nate had a special way of being oblivious. Olivia, however, had a special way of noticing things she wished she didn't. At the sight of Ruth's provocative gesture, Olivia's cheeks pressed up into the edges of her eyes, and her head pitched downward. Olivia wasn't the jealous type, but when it came to Nate, she was.

Foliage ran deep and thick around the back of the house. Knotweed, ragweed, and dogfennel stood lanky, linked into a kind of looming, parasitic shrubbery. Though formidable, its height paled in comparison to the rear wall of the house, which, from where they stood, appeared more like a grand château with the veranda some fifty feet up, the columns of the veranda extending up further.

The opulence of the low country's form—the oaks with their moss curtains, the quilts of yellow powder, the clap of the cicadas—was unparalleled in its terrific splendor. It left you with an unfamiliar peace that was both sublime and terrifying. The South had that uncanny ability of making almost any day look like summer, and on this blistering spring morning, it was especially true. The rich landscape didn't contrast with the eerie visage of the house but rather, somehow illuminated it. It was as though, in some peculiar way, the two complemented one another. Beauty was friend to the vile.

Finding the entrance was still their overarching objective, but, remained unforeseeable. Daphne had gone to check the other side of the mansion and returned with only a shake of her head in her typical jerky fashion.

"There looks to be some differentiation in the stones," Nate said, examining the back wall.

Amir looked to his friends. "Did everyone bring their climbing shoes?"

"I didn't, actually," Olivia joked, hiding her sneakered feet in the grass.

Nate pointed to the base of the wall where, hidden under the knotweed, was a bed of boulders that would split a skull if given the chance. "Don't slip."

2

Finger strength was the name of the game as the crew muscled up the wall. The indentations in the stacked stone provided just an inch of foothold, maybe two. Gaping down at the mouth of rocks ready to swallow any who faltered, the friends realized that the jagged crags seemed much meaner from above.

Grip and breath quickly dissolved among the kids. Though they were all sixteen and headed toward the height of life's physical durability, reaching the peak of the veranda and rolling over the stone railing, was utterly exhausting. But their fatigue slowly morphed to satisfaction as they saw what lay before them. At the other end of the extensive deck—a door that led inside the home. It was not inviting. Black iron ornamentation slithered around its frame, giving it an aura of disdain for all who passed through it.

On either side of the door sat two small cherubim on waist-high obelisks. Whether it was their dying composure or crooked expressions, the little angelic statues told the teenagers this was a place of greatness, of nobility, and of death. The hesitation in the faces of each of the five friends almost began to mirror that of either cherub. Even Ruth looked partially frazzled.

"Well, come on then," she mustered.

Come on then, they did. One after the other into the house, through the glass door with its witch-like embellishment.

Once inside, the air was wet and warm and clotted. It stuck to their skin and lungs, the same as some foul aroma that hooked into their nostrils, both forces shortening their breath. The thick, stone walls trapped the humidity inside them like a vault, and they compounded its weight so that movement in the house was slow and daze-like, and the heat of the day was magnified.

The many elongated windows offered the house more light from the outside than it appeared to possess on the inside. It was as though an invisible filter rested behind each window, stifling the sun.

Amir plucked a decorative box off a table. The casing of the box was chipped and crusted, and suddenly, Amir hurled it at a window. It flew into the double-paned barrier, screeched across the glass, and plummeted back down to the floor. Nate flinched at the sound as Amir wore his typical smirk. No one said anything, either because they were too preoccupied with the oddities of the rest of the place or because they were used to Amir's sudden outbursts.

Tarnished silver bathed in a buttery grime threw back the form of a faded, golden figure. Ruth's wipe smeared the grime away, revealing her as the translucent image in the reflection. Smut collected under her palms and between her fingers. Under the dust, the finely decorated frame was not as lusterless as it had previously seemed. Retaining a considerable shine, the mirror was elegant, and in the reflection,

Ruth posed to appear just as refined. She approved of her likeness with a practiced smile.

They were in the living area, which was infested with an orange, radioactive gloom. Strange and sharp light reflections lurked in from other parts of the house. The light appeared to be further streaks of daylight, yet unmotivated and nonsensical in its pathways. The crumbled walls and furniture made the place look like the inside of a corroded battery. Once again, the contradiction arose that something wasn't right about this place. How could the exterior—regardless of the roping ivy and overgrown vegetation—look so vivid, so well-maintained, and the inside look like this?

Nate thought hard about this, but unlike his counterparts, who were becoming increasingly uneasy, he became increasingly intrigued.

"At least there's no pollen," said Daphne with a scratch.

No one laughed.

"It smells like someone ate rotting flesh and then threw it up," said Ruth.

"Oh, sorry. That was me," said Amir with a smirk.

Ruth rolled her eyes, and Nate smiled a little.

As the group stirred on, the shadows stood heavier, and it was all Olivia could notice. "Anyone else up for keeping their life?"

"You just want to leave because it was my idea to come here," said Ruth.

"I want to leave because in the last room, the fireplace looked like it was designed by the devil. Who carves a mantle in black marble?"

"I think we should keep going," said Daphne, turning to Ruth for validation.

"Nate, you don't want to stay here. Do you?" asked Olivia, grabbing his arm.

He shrugged. "It's an old house. Were you expecting something different when you walked nine miles to get here?"

"Do you not have a weird feeling?"

Nate lied and shook his head.

"She's got a weird feeling all right," said Ruth, her eyes locked on Olivia's grip.

Olivia ejected Nate's arm from her grasp. Her cheeks flushed red as she crossed her arms and pressed her lips together, refraining from opening them with all her strength.

"Olive, you're a cake that hasn't been cut into yet, but once a few slices are missing, you'll be a little less sweet," said Ruth.

"Why don't you shut up for once, Ruth?" Olivia snapped.

"There goes the first slice."

"Okay, let's just everybody cool it. I know that's hard given this house is a kiln, but just try. We all agreed to come here, and here we are. Now, we're going to find this *dark*. We're going to talk to this demon. We're going to worship it a little, give it some words of affirmation, whatever it wants. We're going to learn a little more about ourselves. And then we're getting out. Capiche?" said Amir.

"You still haven't been listening. We are here. That's a feat. But you don't find *the dark*. It finds you," said Ruth.

They continued on through the house. The rooms were large, too large. Each one seemed bigger than the last.

"We were just in the library," said Amir as he emerged from the previous room.

"Is that what that was? I thought it was a dungeon," said Olivia.

"I thought it was a coliseum," said Daphne.

"That's not the library behind us," Amir motioned with his thumb.

Ruth looked around him. "What is it?"

"It's a kitchen."

"You mean the room changed?"

"If it didn't change, then we weren't just in the library."

"But we *were* just in the library," Olivia confirmed with a tremble.

"I know. That's what I'm saying."

"It's playing games," Ruth smiled. "It's testing us. It wants to know if we're worthy of what the dark—and its inhabitant—has to offer."

"So, what's in the dark?" Nate asked calmly. "I mean, what's really in there?"

"The secrets of the universe."

"What if this *demon* doesn't know anything?" said Olivia.

"It might not be a demon. It might be a sage," said Ruth.

"Are we that in need of advice to take the risk? A demon might give you counsel, or it might give you a hand of claws to the throat."

"He who is wise seeks wisdom."

"He who is wise is wise enough to know not to trade more wisdom for his life."

Ruth stepped toward Olivia, encroaching on her space. "Your innocence never ceases to charm us, Olive, but being innocent isn't always wise."

"Ruth, from what you've heard about this place, about *the dark*, this thing hasn't hurt anyone, has it? The demon, I mean," Nate interrupted.

"Would it really matter if it had?" said Ruth. "We've probably done just as much damage as it has, if not more."

"So, it's going to be like 20 Questions?" said Amir.

"More like a fortune teller, at least from what I've heard."

"Everyone needs a fortune teller," Daphne offered, trying to be a part of the conversation.

"Not everyone needs a fortune," muttered Olivia.

The house did not intimidate their curiosity, despite its soggy wretchedness. The sooty wood beneath their sneakers was rotted and mushed in between the grooves of their rubber soles. The labyrinthine nature of the place persisted in its games. One room became a room they'd already been to. Another became the same room they were already in. And so it went for an hour, maybe two.

Nate couldn't tell if it was real or if they only thought it was real. He wasn't sure there was a difference. Then he wanted to try something. Nate imagined a staircase. It was grand, with long curving railings that coiled into spirals at either end. The balustrades were simple: white, cylindrical, and plain. The bannisters atop them were made of elm and painted bold black. Nate wasn't sure he'd ever

21

seen an elm banister. Even if he had, he wasn't sure he could tell the difference between oak or mahogany or elm or take your pick, but he still knew and envisioned it.

As they stepped through the next entryway, the five of them were suddenly in an entirely new room. It was the foyer. A dome skylight crowned its peak, shooting belts of trapezoidal light onto the floor. The foyer was large and made larger by the colossal, grand stairwell sloping up to another floor of the house.

Nate's eyes popped wide, and his stomach was tingly when he saw it. It was the exact same staircase he'd just imagined. Metaphysical to physical manifestation. Had he been here before? Had he previously been to a home designed by the same architect or builder, and therefore, seen a similar, perhaps nearly identical staircase? He could swear he hadn't.

As Nate ran his finger along the banister, feeling the smoothness of the black elm, he beheld the staircase with a certain reverence. There was a lust behind his glance at his *creation*. If for only a split moment, Olivia caught it.

Then a *shrieeeeek* shook Nate, and he snapped his hand off the banister. Amir had a sharp fragment from a broken lamp in his hand and was dragging it along the elm, creating a thin gash in the gloss.

"What are you doing?" Nate snapped with an unusual fierceness.

"Sorry," was all Amir said, putting up a hand and stepping away.

Nate went back to secretly admiring the railing, as Ruth, Amir, and Daphne went up the staircase without over-deliberation. However, Nate got the feeling that Olivia was more terrified than she was letting on. He even thought he spotted a tremor emerging in her sweaty hands. At the back of the pack, those damp palms once again clamped his.

"So, you *did* want to come out here?" asked Olivia.

"What makes you say that?"

"I know you, Nate. I've known you since we were three. I know when you're keeping something from me. Why are you here?"

"Honestly, I can't remember."

Olivia didn't buy it. "So, you're a little lost. It doesn't mean you can't be found. Nate… nothing can be found in the dark."

"Well, I haven't found much in the light either, so I figured it was worth a shot."

"God hasn't shown you what you thought he should yet. Maybe you're not ready."

"I don't know what I need to do to *be* ready, Olivia. That's the whole point."

Ruth's prying glance drifted down from the top of the stairs, watching Nate and Olivia's side conversation.

"What can darkness offer? It has nothing. It *is* nothing."

"I guess I'm just hoping it can offer me more than anyone else in my life has," said Nate, as he stormed up the stairs. The red velvet carpet that was buttoned to the wood was sprinkled with filth and soiled under his stomp.

Inside, he was churning like a monsoon, flushed at the fact that Olivia knew him so well. But then again, he knew, she didn't. Olivia was correct in her pressuring, but wrong in her conclusion. She knew when to prod but never what about.

Olivia's glance moved to Ruth's, which bounced away. Ruth turned to continue up the rest of the stairwell, hiding a brief smile.

The upstairs hall splintered into two separate directions, both expanding deep into the recesses of the mansion, curving off at the ends.

"Split?" said Ruth.

"No," Nate shook his head. "Left."

Ruth smiled at Nate's confidence while Olivia swallowed needles. But Nate wasn't confident in going left; he was confident in his ability to manifest and that no matter which way they went, he could imagine wherever they needed to be, and thus, get them to the dark.

"You act like you've been here before, Nate," Amir noted casually.

"I haven't been here before, but that doesn't mean I don't recognize it."

"You recognize somewhere you've never been?"

"It's called déjà vu."

"No, déjà vu is where you remember a place you *have* been. Here we've been wandering around for as long as we have. We've got water and snacks, but we'll need a lot of it to get back. Unless, of course, you know the way."

"I don't know the way."

"Or you do, and what, you just don't remember?"

Nate despised it when Amir would press like this, and he always pressed like this.

"I never said I don't remember. Look, I'm not sure if I've been here. In fact, I'm almost positive I haven't. But being here feels like I've forgotten something that I don't remember. So, no, I didn't know the way. I *don't* know the way," Nate explained, doing his best to mask the turmoil that was bubbling inside him.

"Natey-Nate. Always with the games. You don't need to show us how smart you are. We already know."

But Nate knew it was Amir who always thought he was smart, Amir who was always with the games, and Nate had about had enough of them. Ruth registered the hue of Nate's face as it grew increasingly red.

"Which way, Nate?" she asked gently, as they reached the end of the hallway, which was a four-way intersection.

"Up." His eyes were settled on another red velvet staircase ascending into snickering shadows. Light reflections from who knows where crawled between the draping tapestries and venerable shields that hung crookedly on the wall at uncanny angles. Way up at the top of the stairwell, dusty, yellow-orange light appeared like a distant and ominous star.

As the features of the home gradually became more off-putting, the contrast in confidence between Nate and his friends became rather stark. Ruth, spooked beyond her usual tenacity, took Nate's hand. He did not refuse, nor did he catch Ruth turning back to ensure Olivia noticed her gesture. Olivia's stare dropped back down to the spotted velvet.

The foreboding star at the top of the stairs was not nearly as gloomy as it had appeared below. Though the house was growing darker the further they traveled, the degree of visibility was still permissible. They passed between a series of smaller rooms. At the end of the sixth room, Nate knew in his heart that a black spiral staircase would be at the end of the seventh. And so, it was.

The pattern with which they migrated about the upper rooms was illogical, which, of course, Amir pointed out. It seemed that although they were progressing, they were simultaneously regressing. Ruth hypothesized to the group that while they believed themselves to be on the far-right side of the house, they were actually on the left. Nate couldn't figure it out, but somehow, he knew she was correct.

They took the spiral staircase up into the attic. Ruth stretched Nate's arm as she held onto him from below, following him up. Nate's shoulder was beginning to bother him because of the awkward curvature of the stairs that caused their bodies to contort slightly. Regardless, he kept Ruth's hand in his. He did this not so much because he liked Ruth or because he wanted to lead on to her affection, but because he preferred to keep Olivia at a distance. He needed to concentrate.

The first room at the top of the stairs was only about six or seven feet long and soiled like the others. Leading out of it was a substantial entryway to a much larger room—the largest in the house by a significant margin. Nate knew this was it. He no longer had to imagine. He no longer had to fight the labyrinth-like thinking of the mansion. His manifesting became second nature. These halls were his own.

The five friends stepped through the massive frame together, and each entered a momentary state of paralysis. A fear overtook them—their eyes were screaming, their swallows hardening, their foreheads dripping, and their bodies shaking. A chill slithered into their veins. This room was noticeably cooler than the rest of the house. The smell was not putrid or dead like the lower levels. Instead, the aroma was of vanilla and honeysuckle and cherry blossom. Hints of clove and spice and mint teased in the recesses. The scents, fair temperature, and wholeness of the air were intoxicating.

The room was mammoth in scale. It was too large to be the attic, but based on its placement inside the home's structure, there wasn't much else it could be. The bacterial pink walls peeled and slit in jags. The rosy wallpaper surrounded something black, something darker than black, something diabolical. The stunted leers of each of the five kids locked onto it like magnets, as if they had no choice, horrified by the ornate molding around it, yet craving what skulked inside. It was an open doorway with no door or hinges and no sign that it had ever possessed either. Behind the doorway was utter, cruel blackness. No light came in. None came out. They all knew with absolute and distasteful certainty that this was *the dark.*

Four squares of sun privileged the puddled floor, sectioned by a slanted shadow cross. They came from a square window that was four feet by four feet with two pieces of overlapping iron trim barring the outside of the glass. The window offered the only real brightness to the attic. Nate recognized it as the same window he'd seen from the courtyard.

3

No one could say how long they stayed there, standing in place. It could've been seconds. It could've been minutes or longer. They stood and waited, knowing they could move closer but deciding instead to marvel and behold like a vulture waiting for its meal to die.

Ruth spoke first. "Who wants the honors?"

"Don't you?" Amir glanced over.

"I thought so, but…"

"I didn't know darkness could be so bright," said Daphne from nowhere.

Ruth perched in place a few moments longer. Finally, she inched toward the doorway, toward *the dark*. The blackness seemed to punch out, like some metaphysical rage, like a thousand swords of hate. After a deep breath, Ruth was gone, inside the abyss.

Amir, Daphne, and Olivia waited with clenched fists, squeezing cool sweat back into their skin. Their tight natures contrasted with Nate's entirely, who was calm and moderate.

"How long has it been?" Olivia asked worriedly.

"Like three seconds," said Amir.

"At what point do we go in and rescue her?"

"You would rescue Ruth?"

"If I had to."

"We haven't heard any screams yet. Once we hear screams, then I'll start to get worried."

"Depends on the scream," said Daphne with a faint smirk. Her nails flashed to her forearm and scratched.

For a second at least, Nate agreed with Olivia's thinking, and then, he didn't. It was surreal to him—all of this, this place. It beckoned to him. The doorway and the dark churning inside it mirrored the gates of Hell, but to Nate, that did not make it any less enticing. He wanted *the dark*. He wanted to feel it. He wanted to submerge in it. For some reason, which he couldn't quite track, he coveted *the dark* and deeply believed it would heal him.

Ruth stepped back into the light of the attic. There was no shock in her gaze, nor even a hint of incredulity. It was, strangely, a restrained harmony. Nate wondered if anyone but him saw it or if they happened to catch the sick grin that was stuck to her face the instant she emerged from the blackness.

"You look okay," Amir said, eyeing her.

But Nate knew she didn't. She seemed wiser. A new understanding stood behind her glacial blue eyes, the kind you never shake, the kind even electroshock therapy couldn't reverse. It was a knowing understanding. She had seen something in the dark she would never forget, but Nate knew she wouldn't want to. He knew that the truth could be heavier than the world, but that sometimes we liked to feel the pressure.

He considered how, at times, there'd been glimpses of darkness in Ruth—trenches in her soul that she kept locked away, beyond her usual overbearing and manipulative self. It was as though in this moment she had never been more herself, and she knew it. She embraced the twisted parts of herself, as a fisherman embraces a catch that he knows he can't reel in. For some reason, again, which he couldn't understand, it was a burden Nate thirsted for.

While the others studied Ruth's refreshed expression, Olivia studied Nate. She saw that he appeared to be looking in Ruth's direction, but really, he was looking past her. Nate's gaze was latched onto the dark.

"Well," said Daphne.

"It's dark," said Ruth.

Amir, unable to control himself, said, "How many dimensions are there? Are we living in a false reality? How old are you going to live to be? How—"

"It's nothing. It's empty."

"And the demon?"

"It feeds on consciousness," Ruth said, suddenly turning pale.

"Feeds on consciousness?"

Her breaths grew fuller, "It was strange. It wanted to know things that it already knew. It wanted to make sure I knew them. It wanted to taste the words in my mouth. It wanted to say them with me."

Nate hung on Ruth's every word. He began to salivate.

"It feeds on consciousness, and in return, it serves wisdom. I don't feel so good."

Nate became perplexed at Ruth's sudden change in demeanor. He couldn't tell if it was real or if she only wanted him to think it was real.

"Please. Did it tell you to say all that?" Amir said with a cheap laugh. He took a sliver of wood and slung it into the dark. It didn't make a sound. It didn't drop. It simply vanished. He strode up to the doorway that towered over him. As he craned his neck up at the macabre frame and squinted into the void, his *courage* looked a little more like trepidation. Poking an arm in to test the waters, the darkness clung to his skin the way a beggar clings to money.

Ruth dripped down the wall to join the puddles on the floor, bringing clumps of crusted spores and bits of pink plaster along with her. Daphne was attentive to her master as always and did her best to dust off the flecks from Ruth's bunched-up shirt. Despite her irritation, Olivia knelt and did the same. As she dusted Ruth erratically, she nearly sent her glasses sailing off again.

Daphne stared into the hollowness of Ruth's dark gaze that presented her with a wraith-like aura—ghostly and slightly divine. Nate wondered if this was some sort of side effect of the experience. *Was it like caffeine?* He thought. *Hits you with a high, then jabs you with a low.* He wondered how long the low would last.

Amir was inside before anyone knew he'd left. He would do that occasionally. One minute you couldn't get rid of him, the next you couldn't find him.

Nate planted in the center of the room, gaze still locked onto the doorway, leeching into the black. Its intoxicating intrigue did not desist.

"How was it? Really?" Daphne asked, excitement in her voice.

"You should try it. It'll take your breath away," Ruth simply giggled. "But there was something else.

I can't quite remember." Her glance flicked to Nate for a split second, and then shot back to the rotted floorboards.

Daphne turned back to the hellish entryway to catch Amir easing out of it. He carried that same blank expression that Ruth did.

"That was a trip."

"What kind of trip?" asked Nate.

"The kind where you have the time of your life, but at the end, you know you're ready to come home."

That sounded like Hell, if anything, to Nate. But it didn't scare him. It excited him, the way alcohol sometimes did. But what was so exciting about it? He was trying harder than ever to pinpoint just that. Hell was not an alluring place, as far as he'd heard. So then, this couldn't be Hell, yet it—so far—possessed all qualities of it. The black doorway, *the dark*, was a standing contradiction, an invitation of both desire and desperation.

"Is it the gate to Hell?" said Nate.

"Worse."

"Worse?"

"Worse," said Amir, and he propped himself with one arm against the window and sucked the room's dust into his lungs.

Worse? What could *worse* mean? Nate wanted more than ever to leap through that doorway, but something stopped him. His faith had two hands on his shoulders and was wrenching him back. God was there, whispering in his ear, telling him to turn back, to listen to Olivia. Nate could hardly fathom that the Lord had followed him to this wretched place, this place where the smell of sour mildew clamped to the inside of your nostrils and the damp air crawled into your throat like flies. Wasn't God too high and mighty to be in a place like this? Wouldn't He be too upset that Nate wasn't praising Him instead? Well, God may be even *here*, but God had his chance. Nate was after something, something more in his life, some further experience.

Surely, Amir was only joking, and he could be a master joker when he wanted to be, sometimes even a cruel one. Nate recollected how once, in seventh grade, Amir had climbed up and stood on top of the sink counter in the boys' bathroom. He then—from his leveraged position—proceeded to urinate into the hand drying unit next to the sink. The moment someone pressed that button, the interior fans would disperse urine about the room like a mosquito mister. Of course, some poor soul fell for it. They knew because the bathroom reeked for nearly two weeks.

Amir laughed about it for months after. Nate laughed at first, but then considered the custodial staff that had to scrub it up and the kid who probably ruined his favorite shirt. Nate didn't know why Amir did it. He had only found out about it after the fact when Amir told him. No one saw Amir do it. No one knew about it except for Nate. Therefore, if his corrupt actions weren't for attention, as most pranks naturally were, what was it for? The idea of a prank is that you parade into the spotlight after and take credit for what you did as a sort of magician or clever genius who was smart enough to foresee something that someone else wasn't. Your planning, your preparation were, in a way, rewarded.

Could he have done it for the laugh? But who was that desperate for a smile? Who was willing enough to cause someone suffering for a smirk? No. What was the cause? Nate had pondered it for days. There was something underneath. But despite Amir's history of jokes, Nate knew his current state of disorder, his cluttered stoicism, was no act.

Though he didn't necessarily *enjoy* seeing his friends in distress, he at times considered himself something of a psychologist. Nate had an innate sense and a certain comprehension of the psyche, and thus, was steadfast in his desire to decode the source of both Amir's internal turmoil and Ruth's secret delight. It occupied his thoughts as much as the dark, which he was preparing to descend, which he was dying to descend.

"You want it?" said Daphne with a flinch.

"You don't seriously think I'm going in there?" said Olivia.

Daphne shrugged.

"But I am trying to figure out why you are," said Olivia. "I still don't understand you, Daph. You've already taken so much of yourself. Can't you leave the rest?"

Daphne crunched her face and pressed her eyes into a tight squint directed at Olivia. Her teeth locked, and her jaw bulged out of her cheeks.

"I'm sure Nate will come to his senses. Why don't you?" said Olivia.

"I'm not sure I have any sense to come to. I find that makes life a little easier," said Daphne, her neck muscles jutting.

"Why do you always have to know everything? Maybe life's meant to be a mystery."

"It *is* meant to be a mystery, and I'm meant to solve it. It's why I'm here."

"You're here because she's here." Olivia nodded to Ruth.

"Oh, I see. You think if I go in that door, it's not because I want to but because somebody told me to."

"I think that no matter what you think you want, you have to go in there. I've been telling Nate, Daph, if you want freedom, that's the last place you should look."

Daphne was seething. You could almost see the blood in her veins boiling. Her face was molten red, and her jawline was practically tearing through the skin. "My turn," she said.

As Daphne shot up and sprang toward the door, her manner shifted. At once subduing fury, now she was hiding reluctance and fear. Nate noticed how her cheeks flushed, how her swallow was tight, how her nose scrunched.

He discerned little things like this. Nate had this sixth sense about people. A different degree of consciousness was how he saw it—a higher degree. His perception of human nature was more adept than even he'd prefer. It was as if he knew a person before he knew them. He could talk with someone he'd just met for only a minute or so, or see them converse with someone else, and he knew in an instant whether or not they could get upset, how upset they could get, whether or not they could cry, whether or not they could wail, or whether or not they would ever be happy.

His observation continued as Daphne trudged toward the dark. He knew, he knew in his pounding heart, she would refrain. Then, to his surprise, Daphne nailed her eyelids shut and stepped into the dark.

The four of them all sat glued to the tall doorway, menacing in its stature, its serpent teeth gnashing out, hungry to devour. None of them were properly prepared to go beyond, into whatever sinister realm this dark supposedly was, but Daphne least of all.

She was in there longer than both her predecessors. The minutes rolled by carefully. Much to the puzzled dismay of Olivia and Amir, Daphne was giggly when she materialized from the thick shadows. She looked as high as hot air, as though her head was filled with it. *What could make her feel like this?* Nate thought. Amir distraught, Ruth distorted, and now, Daphne elated. What was the demon playing at? What did the dark know? What would it soon show him? Would he soon have the answers he so desperately sought? Before he could break from his thoughts, he stumbled backward to find Daphne wrapped tightly around him, squeezing him so his insides squished over each other.

"Daphne," Nate said gently. She held. "Daphne," he said again with more force.

Olivia pried her off. Daphne hardly resisted before she latched onto Olivia with the same grip. Amir stepped in now. With Nate's help, they tore her off and flung her backwards. Daphne looked past the three of them into the distance on the opposite side of the attic. A distant smile slept between her cheeks.

Nate caught Ruth's glance digging into him. She was still over by the far wall, standing now, with that sick grin plastered on her face once again. The grin was quiet so as not to catch the attention of the others, but intentional enough to address Nate. The grin burrowed into his stomach. He wasn't afraid of it, or of Ruth. He was too preoccupied with deciphering its purpose.

"Olivia," Nate finally muttered.

"You still think this is the place to find your purpose?" she said.

"Have you decided to go in? Or is it my turn?"

"If you think I'm letting you go in there, you're as crazy as her." She nodded to Daphne, still gazing stonily into the ether.

"I've come all this way."

Olivia pulled him aside. "That doesn't mean you have to go any further. Don't you see what's happening?"

"You don't think it's real. You don't think there's anything behind that door."

"Nate, I know it's real. But you need to understand, I can't let anything happen to you."

"Why?"

"I'll only tell you if you don't go in."

"Olivia, I think if I don't walk through that door, I'll never be the person I'm supposed to be."

"You're exactly the person you're supposed to be. Right now. And I will do anything not to lose that. People can change, Nate, but not always for the better. You're going to find that this is where you belong, not in there."

"How can we find ourselves if we aren't lost first?"

"You've already been found."

With his index finger, Nate gently pushed back Olivia's glasses, which were sliding down the bridge of her nose, and then broke away from her. He positioned himself in the center of the room, square with the blackened doorway. As he marched forward, Amir placed a gentle hand on his shoulder to pause him for a moment.

"Don't, Nate," said Amir. "There's nothing to find in there that you'll be glad you discovered."

"We've always had differences in taste."

"Something's off, man. Don't do it. You know when I'm being serious. I don't feel right. I don't feel the same. I don't feel I'll ever be the same."

"All that from a few minutes with a demon?"

"It's not a demon."

Nate just stared at his friend for a moment. Finally, Amir lowered his hand from Nate's shoulder and stepped aside. Nate swallowed, took a breath in like it was his last, readied himself, and—

"Remember, Nate, don't stay too long. We're gone by sunset," Amir warned.

"I'm not afraid of the dark." Nate set forth into it.

4

Inside, there was no light. It was all black. Even the doorway that he'd just passed through was gone. There was nothing behind him except utter darkness. Nate wasn't afraid. In fact, he felt comfortable. The air was fair and cool and tingly as it wrapped itself around his body. It made him alert, energized, as though the particles gave off an electrical emission. The hairs on Nate's arms stood for a moment and then sat back down.

Though he couldn't see, he could sense that *the dark* was nothing more than a room, perhaps a small corridor some seventeen feet long. Not big but not small either. As he was getting a feel for the space, that's when he saw it step into the light, except there was no light to step into. It more or less manifested the dark, adjusted to it as Nate had adjusted to the shape that emerged at the other side of the room. It didn't take a specific form but appeared to have a scaly, dark exterior—skin, you could call it—slid over the form of a man-like being. Its eyes were edged and whetted. They were mustard yellow like a cat, but less curious and more intentional and more human, even. The eyes were hypocritical. They at once sparkled like full moonlight, and then behind the sparkle, they felt piercing and jagged. Appearance-wise, there was no mistaking it for a demon, but it held a surprisingly casual and unpretentious demeanor.

It was wise. Nate could tell it was wise. He processed the demon as the demon processed him. They studied one another, neither ready to begin the conversation. Nate, growing impatient—

"Do you know why I'm here?" Nate asked. The utterance startled him because he realized he hadn't yet opened his mouth.

"I suspect you know that I do," said the demon without opening its own. It spoke with a guttural rasp. The speech was devilishly confident and possessed a sneaking echo that clattered about.

"How is this possible?"

"Us speaking without the usage of our lips?"

"Yeah."

"Your limited perception has led you to believe much of what is possible is not when in fact it is," responded the demon. His tongue slithered.

"What is this place?"

"I can show you what you want to know, about life, about yourself, not that you are prepared to see it."

"You plan to enlighten me?"

"That is what you wish, yes?"

"I find it hard to believe a person could be *enlightened* in a place like this."

"I understand how you feel, but this is the only place one can be enlightened."

"What do you mean?"

"I know why you are here. You want to know the answer to the question: Who am I? But do you really think you will find it by searching for what is not hiding? To learn a person's true character is valuable, and what is valuable is hard to obtain. Anyone can see what sits in the light. It is plain. It is open. It is available. But few ever realize what is lurking in its enemy."

"Well, then. Here I am."

"Yes. Here you are. Here *we* are. Now, a question. Does one choose to be enlightened? Or does it suddenly come upon them?"

"I guess, they don't choose it."

"Exactly."

"But yet I chose to be here."

"That you did, but you did not choose what being here would mean."

"I knew what I wanted it to mean."

"That carries influence, certainly, but I have my own way of doing things. As we proceed, it is important that you not let fear step between us."

"I'm not afraid of the dark, or of you."

"No, you are not afraid of the dark. Otherwise, you would not have made it this far. But you will be afraid of the truth. And Nathan, I am the truth."

Amir, Daphne, Ruth, and Olivia all stood and stared at the hollow doorway in total silence. They saw no indentation of Nate's figure in the black, not a hint of a silhouette. They heard nothing of the conversation between Nate and the demon.

"He's been in there a minute," Amir shook his head.

Ruth shrugged. "He's having a good time. I did."

"I don't like this," said Olivia.

"You don't like anything. When was the last time you actually embraced something that we've done?"

"I embraced *this*. Sorry, but I'm no longer endorsing it."

"Oh, sure, you embraced it, and you complained the whole way here. Let me ask you something, Olive. Have you ever done anything besides worry?"

"I'm sorry that I care about Nate."

"You're probably even more sorry that he doesn't care as much about you."

Olivia tucked her chin as her glance smacked the floor, averting Ruth's.

"Lay off, Ruth," said Amir.

"What time is it?"

As if summoned, "Almost three. He's got plenty of time," said Daphne, still somewhat in a daze.

"What do we do?" said Olivia.

"We don't do anything. We wait," said Ruth.

After another long silence, Amir spoke up and said, "So, are we going to talk about what we saw in there? What Nate's seeing now."

"You looked spooked, Amir," said Ruth.

"You didn't."

"Perhaps we didn't see the same thing."

"Olivia, how long would you say each of us was in there?"

"You were in there for ten minutes, maybe. Ruth was in there for about fifteen. Daphne was in there for twenty or twenty-five."

"Still feeling tough, Amir? After you got outlasted by girls," Ruth poked.

"I'm not sure I even know what tough means anymore."

"What's in there?" said Olivia.

"Put it like this, Nate's going to have issues if he ever comes out," said Daphne, who laughed and then jerked her hand to scratch her arm.

"If you don't want to stain your veil of purity, I wouldn't go in. Not that you have the guts to," said Ruth.

After a moment—

"What did you see?" said Ruth to Amir.

He said nothing for a few minutes.

"What did you see, Amir?" repeated Olivia calmly.

"Eyes."

"What?"

"Eyes," Ruth butted in.

"I still see them," said Amir. "That piercing red."

"Red? They weren't red."

"They were red."

"No, they were green."

"They were green," Daphne stammered.

Amir sighed. "The experience must be subjective. The demon sees something different in each of us. Some different route of manipulation."

"It deceived you, but I was the one deceiving it."

"What did it tell you?"

"What I needed to know. In a way, what I already knew."

"What's that?"

The sneaky smile returned to Ruth's face. It did not fear being seen. "The way I'll become the woman I'm to become. I was missing a few steps that I now know. I think Nate will have a similar experience."

"Why do you say that?" said Olivia.

"Because he was the one who wanted to come here."

Amir and Olivia turned to one another in perplexity, their crinkled squints matching.

"He was," Daphne giggled.

"You wanted to come here," Amir tried to clarify.

"I did, but it was Nate's idea. He's the one who told me about this place," said Ruth.

"What do you mean he told you? Everyone knows about this place."

"Yes, but he was the one who knew how to get here."

5

"You are depressed," said the demon.

Its gaze never wavered from Nate, never broke, and never blinked. Those devil yellow eyes sat in the absolute black, about the same height as Nate's, level with his, that now studied the floor they couldn't see. The yellow was stark and paint-like and exuded every flavor of both destruction and preservation. They despised Nate, and they desired him.

"I've lost a part of myself. I'm not even sure exactly what it is. I just know that I want to find it again," said Nate.

"Perhaps you have not lost a part of yourself but rather have not found a part yet."

"How do I escape emptiness? How do I find purpose?"

"It is difficult to reach a destination without a map. It is equally difficult when the captain sails knowingly into the storm."

"It feels like my senses have dulled, like I'm only half alive."

"You are a man of God."

"Does that surprise you?"

"It should surprise you."

"And you think a man of God shouldn't feel like this?"

"If you have come *here* to save your faith, there must not be much to save."

"Maybe I have a purpose, but I don't care about what that purpose is. And I don't know why I don't care. I feel nothing. I know it doesn't matter what I feel, and that truth and logic are absolute. I know I should follow God regardless. I know I don't have to feel anything to serve him and move forward. I can move forward even if I don't feel alive. But at the same time, I can't."

"And you thought, perhaps, I could make you care again."

"No priest or pastor could answer my questions."

"It is possible that I can, but I must first know more of you before you can know more."

"Such as?" Nate stood in the face of this malicious, metaphysical creature and jeered at it as if it were a school friend.

"Let's talk about your father."

"Ask me about something else."

"Unfortunately, I cannot. Your father is a large part of the reason why you are here."

"What do you know about him?"

"More than you, you will see."

"So, I'm supposed to confront what you know?"

"In a way, yes."

At the mention of his father, in his mind, Nate immediately went back to a July day in the baking heat of the Carolina summer. The times he spent with his father were often disassociated or disconnected. Either from the incessant errands before arriving at the thing his father originally promised they would do, or from his father's inability to detach from work, their interactions typically lay on the edge of meaningless. On this particular evening, Nate's father was taking him to a baseball game and dinner. The local minor team, the Road Rabbits, who somehow managed to pull sell-out crowds, were squaring off against the Sidewinders.

Nate wondered if his father even knew how little he cared about baseball. It was America's pastime, and Nate hoped that eventually, people would get the message. He also wondered why minor league sports always selected degenerate animals as their mascots, as if to hurl every possible insult at the players for just missing their shot at the big leagues and serving as a constant reminder that they're only second best. They weren't bears or tigers. They were bunny rabbits and sidewinder rattlesnakes. This was a corrupt thought, and Nate knew it. Some of these men were proud, some of them were able to financially support their families, at least to a degree, all for playing a kid's game. Nate sometimes had a cruelty in his belly, a distaste for certain things. He didn't know where it came from or why it would suddenly arise at the seemingly most random moments. Was it his father? Was it jealousy for these men? Did he actually like baseball and not know it? No one ever saw the more aggressive side of Nate's thoughts. He hardly did himself. But they were nonetheless there, and they came from somewhere.

While at dinner, Nate thought more about his mental deviations than about what his father was lecturing him on—something about the many kinks in the credibility of the theory of evolution. Nate didn't care but was impressed that his father ordered him a plain vanilla milkshake. He might not know he hated baseball, but he could remember a lousy milkshake. Nate supposed that counted for something.

He accepted this get-together offer from his father partly because he had no other plans—a fourteen-year-old never had plans on a Thursday night in the middle of summer—and partly because he clung to some distant hope, some twinkle in the thick sky that they might bond over something. He hoped, truly he hoped, that this evening, and their interaction, wouldn't carry its usual staleness.

Often when he spoke to his father, whether it was a lunch or a car ride or just in passing conversation, Nate knew he had his father's attention for about twenty seconds. Twenty seconds was all it took for his father's mind to walk away to his health, to his finances, or to his work. So, if Nate ever really had something to say, he knew he had better say it quick. The moment arose, and Nate gasped for words. He prayed for something to say, but nothing came. Instead of speaking, his lips shot for the red straw that pumped his mouth with the cold, sweet, milky ice of the vanilla shake. He trickled the back of his fingernail along the ridges of the fountain glass, cutting through the film of condensation. He realized he hardly knew this man whom he'd seen and spoken to practically every day of his life. Nate discovered that in order to create a connection with someone it didn't matter how many hours you'd spent together or even that you *knew* them—and Nate knew more than he wished to know about his father—all that mattered was that you cared, and Nate's stomach was as full of apathy as it was with creamy vanilla milkshake.

"You even remember how it tastes," said the demon, snapping Nate back to reality, back to the dark.

"How what tastes?" Nate asked with unease.

"The milkshake."

Nate's blood flashed cold. His skin writhed, its hairs standing tight. How did it know that? Could it read his mind? Certainly. It just had. If it could see his past, perhaps it could see his future. Then again, Nate thought about how he also possessed such a mind-gauging quality, how he could almost read people's thoughts, how he almost knew what they would do even before they did. Regardless, Nate wasn't good enough to pinpoint a specific memory inside someone else's head, and, as a result, his goosebumps were building goosebump factories.

"How do you have access to what I'm thinking?"

"You let me in. I presented the doorway, and you brought me through it. The priests and pastors and mentors and wise teachers cannot answer your questions because they do not understand," said the demon.

"Why don't they understand?"

"Because your journey is unique, something they have never come across before and will never come across again, even though it sits before them on nearly every page of scripture."

"I've always felt that I was destined for something."

"Many *feel* destined, but few are."

"What separates the chosen from the forgotten?"

"We will get to that, but we must first address your father."

"I don't want to talk about my father."

"Why not?"

"He has nothing to do with my future, only my past."

"Your past creates your future without you knowing."

"Well, if I don't need to know, then we can move on."

"Your mother—"

"My mother's the exact same. Talking about my parents is as much a dead end as being with them is."

"They are controlling you. You have been too blind to see it."

"How?"

"Because they do not even see it. They control you because they need to, because of their own insecurities."

"All my decisions I make on my own."

In that instance, a slash of gleaming white split the darkness below the yellow, murderous eyes. It was a heinous and devious smirk. The demon's grin sparkled with silver and white like stars. It was intelligent, arrogant even, but collected.

"Your parents, in helping you, have defeated you. In trying to save you, they destroyed you. They should have killed you. Then, you'd still be alive."

"If not for their support, then I wouldn't be here. Would I?"

"No, you would not."

"Then they're saving me was necessary to become my fullest and truest self."

"Yes. You are correct," said the demon dismissively, "But you are not correct in assuming their support did not hamper your abilities, did not stall your progress."

"It needed to stall. Otherwise, I'd be somebody else."

"That is exactly my point. Would you be someone else? Or would you be more yourself? Would you have learned on your own? Would you be further progressed than you are presently?"

Nate finally took a moment to absorb the situation he was in. Up to this point, he had not consciously recognized the strangeness of the present reality. He thought for a moment that he and this demon might be friends under alternate circumstances. This was the most rewarding conversation he'd had in years. It's a shame it was with such a foul creature. Nate could not deny the intellect of the demon or its passion toward comprehension, which were both significant. Nate knew he too possessed the rare, indelible assets of both a high IQ and EQ. In fact, he had not encountered another being, human or otherwise, in his entire short existence that matched his own, until now.

I wonder if it'll tell me what I want to know, thought Nate. *I wonder if I can read its thoughts*. Nate's mind flashed with the truth he'd buried in the darkness of his own thoughts. Though he was unsure of this place, this *dark*, Nate knew the secrets of achieving his desires lay here, lay behind those thinking yellow eyes. He knew what he wanted was beyond purpose. It was beyond caring. Nate wanted something far greater, but he wondered if the demon knew that. He wondered if he could trick the demon, if he could trap it. Then, something odd struck Nate. For some reason, he could not release the idea that what if, somehow, it was not *he* who had come to this place, but rather, the demon who came to him. It was known that Nate wanted what the demon kept in the shadows, the truth he begged for. But he also wondered, with a trickle of fear, he wondered if the demon wanted something from him.

Light slowly depleted from the attic. The weary sun hitting the glass of the barred window began its descent, and the black shadow cross on the rotted floor angled northeast, toward that wretched doorway. The space likewise drained of its original blissful scent. The stench of sweat coated the old smell of cinnamon and vanilla and exotic divines. It hung in the nostrils of the four friends producing it, now tired and slouched against the growth-lathered walls. Olivia was the only one still spritely, if only slightly. She paced. Her worried head flicked from the window and the sun outside it to the black doorway, over and over again in an endless loop. "It's getting late. Someone should go in there."

"Amir can handle it," said Ruth.

"I'm not going back in there. In fact, I don't want to stay here any longer. I can't stand looking at that thing for another minute," said Amir. The depths of the dark within the charred frame sucked in his gaze, which couldn't break from it.

"Amir, please," pleaded Olivia.

"I can't. I'm sorry, Olivia. If Nate's been in there this long, he may not be coming back out."

"He's coming back out!" Olivia said with more force than she was expecting.

"You want him back so much, you go in there," said Ruth.

"What I'm trying to figure out is why you don't."

Amir looked at her. "What's wrong, Ruth? I thought it was such a rewarding experience. I thought you'd be dying to go back in."

"I would go back in, but I don't need to," Ruth smirked incandescently.

"I'll go," said Daphne.

"This isn't about getting some rush, Daph," said Olivia. "Don't think we can't see that concealer on your arms."

Daphne snapped her arms to a fold and shuddered.

"Why'd you come out so quickly?" Amir asked.

"What? I was in there the longest," said Daphne.

"Not compared to Nate. If it was so great, why'd you come out at all?"

"I came out because I couldn't handle it anymore."

"You were laughing."

"We all have different tolerance levels. For both pain and pleasure."

Daphne lingered toward the rectangular void when—

"Daphne," said Olivia, grabbing Daphne's arm. "We need to get Nate out."

"I'll find him," she said as the darkness swallowed her body.

In the total blackness, Daphne felt her way through the space. A tiny smile rested on her face. The euphoria of whatever these shadows brought her was evident in that hint of a grin. She kept feeling about, moving her way onward through the corridor. She thought that it felt larger than before, different—colder, perhaps—than how she remembered. In the dim illumination, sparsely dispersed specks were visible on the inside of her elbows. She glanced down, puzzled, and flipped them over. Her smile and the butterflies in her belly evaporated as she noticed something ahead—a traced outline in the emptiness. It was Nate.

"Nate… Nate… Nate?"

Getting closer to him, the lack of giddiness in her chest shifted, hardening with alarm. As she curved around him, the sight was almost too much to bear. She turned her head to the side to avoid staring at him directly. What she saw turned her veins to ice. Nate *was there*, Daphne thought, but at the same time, *he wasn't*. He looked faded, grayed, like a phantom. His hollow eyes beamed straight ahead, ceasing to acknowledge her as though she weren't there.

"Nate." Daphne's eyes began to spill tears. She stepped closer to him, carefully. As she did, a tear plummeted into the pit around her feet, then another. "Nate, we need to leave. Now."

She tried to reach for him but found she couldn't. It wasn't that her arm wouldn't move. It was that she couldn't muster the strength to produce the thought that would control it. She felt like she was in a dream where she wanted more than anything in the world to awaken, but couldn't.

Then, there was something else, something behind her, deeper in the room. She could sense it watching her.

"Nate," she said through soft tears, "Nate, please."

Daphne couldn't turn to face what was perched behind her. She didn't need to. She could feel its vile breathing as her own simpered. The foul air smelled of singed hair and burnt flesh. A million thoughts galloped through her mind. Her heart cracked and banged against her ribs. The tears in her twitching eyes poured steadily, now. Her skin felt suffocatingly tight as if it was being stretched. Her frosted sweat barreled heavily back into her pores, weighing her down. Her mind raced and roared. She searched for a thought, for *the* thought, for—

Daphne toppled out of the dark back into the attic. She clattered to the floor in a sprawl. Her eyes slowly lifted upward to her three friends standing over her. On their faces brewed a mixture of shock, angst, and fear. Even Ruth's jaw bolted back, her teeth making an audible grinding sound. Her eyes struggled to fence the liquid distress they wanted so desperately to unchain.

It wasn't Daphne's demeanor that was so startling, even though terror was glued into her gaze. It was the stark change in her physical appearance. Her clothes were soiled, her skin oily and clogged and spotted. It seemed more likely that she'd returned from a pig farm or a five-day hike in the Everglades than an empty room. Even though she had not been gone more than a minute, Daphne looked wilted, as though she hadn't had food or water in days.

6

Amir bore the bulk of Daphne's weight with her right arm slung over his shoulders. Her body tilted and curled forward. Exhaustion anchored her eyelids down so that she could hardly keep them open. Olivia carefully pitched water to her crusted lips, which were struggling to accept the fluid. Most of it dribbled down her chin and fell into the musty puddles on the floor. With a lame hand, Daphne slapped the bottle away.

In between her sputtering breaths, she muttered, "Nate... we need... we need to help Nate."

"We're going to get help for you and for Nate," said Amir.

"We... we need... to do something... fast."

Ruth gauged the sun on a collision course for the horizon. "You're right about that." She prepared for flight, jamming supplies back into the backpacks they'd brought for the journey. Granola bars, cheese crackers, peanut butter and marshmallow puff sandwiches, apples, bananas, and half a dozen water bottles. It was a hike coming out here, and it would be a fight back for help.

"Amir, help me with the other bag."

"Take her," said Amir, as he transferred Daphne's weight to Olivia.

Olivia continued to funnel water down Daphne's parched throat, her arid tongue never seeming to moisten, her fusty breath not relenting its stench. Daphne placed a hand on Olivia's, signaling her to break.

"Olivia," Daphne said as water pooled off her lower lip.

"Get it down. We don't have that much left," said Olivia.

"Olivia."

"What?"

"Something's wrong."

"Something's wrong? You should see yourself right now. You'd know you didn't need to tell me that."

"This place... isn't what it appears. I think... it releases things that... we've been hiding. The more we have to hide... the more fuel for its fire. I saw him, Olivia."

"Saw who? Nate?"

Daphne nodded.

"Is he okay?"

Daphne shook her head with dismay.

"Did he say anything?"

"He looked... off. It's like he was... *changing*."

"Changing?"

"And there was someone else in there."

"The demon? Was it the same one you saw?"

"I didn't turn around... but that's... just it. When I went in the first time... there wasn't anything there. It was just an empty... dark... cold room."

"But the demon? You said it had green eyes."

"Ruth said it had green eyes. So... I said the same. The thing is, Liv... there were no eyes."

"Then, why did you come out laughing?"

"I have no idea. I guess I was… relieved."

"I'll take her, now," said Amir, wrangling Daphne back over his shoulder. He waddled to the other side of the attic and the iron spiral staircase that corkscrewed down into the house.

"You ready?" said Ruth, as she strapped on a backpack.

"I'm staying," said Olivia.

Overhearing from the other side of the room, Amir skidded to a halt. "You're what?" His voice sounded distant and echoey.

"He's choosing to stay in there. He's choosing to take that risk. You don't owe him anything," said Ruth.

"What if I do?" said Olivia.

"He tricked us all into coming here."

"We all came willingly, especially you, Ruth."

"I didn't know what this place was really capable of." Ruth glanced over her shoulder at Daphne. She was strung out, drooping, a split end. "I didn't believe. Nate was the one who convinced me."

"What happened to her in there?"

"It must be another rule that no one told us about. Rule Number 5: Once someone's in the dark, no one else can interfere. They can only come out on their own."

"What if the rules aren't real? What if he'll be okay, even if he stays in there?"

"So far, the rules have been more than real, and this place is much worse than we imagined."

They stood in silence for a moment when eventually—

"Do you love him?" said Ruth.

"Would you let me have him if I did?"

"You really want a boyfriend who's going to drag you to places like this? You're as twisted as him."

"Let's go!" Amir shouted.

Ruth handed Olivia several water bottles.

"Don't lose sight of that sky. It's 5:37. At 8:15, the second the Sun hits the horizon, you head for that stairwell, and you get out of this house, with or without Nate."

"Will you send help?"

"I'll come back with help. I promise. Olivia, listen to me. At 8:43, something's going to come out of that door, and I want you to be prepared. It might not be Nate. It might look like Nate. It might sound like him. But it might not be him."

"What did you see in there?"

"I think if I told you, you wouldn't stay here, even for Nate."

"Ruth. What did you see in there?"

"8:15."

7

The two spoke for what felt like months to Nate. He began to understand his predicament. He hadn't yet decided what the demon sought from him, but he knew that for whatever reason, his will was bending. He knew that he could leave at any moment, as the demon had told him several times, but with each passing second, he believed the likelihood of his escaping this place decreased drastically. The reason wasn't the demon. Well, not exactly. It was him.

Nate became so engrossed in his discussion with the demon that he honestly thought he could go on talking with it for days. It understood him. That—more than anything else in this odd place—was what surprised Nate the most. He knew of two sure things in life. The first was that you would die. The second and possibly more important—and more gut-wrenching—was that no one would ever understand you.

People could sympathize with you, some could even empathize with you, but in the end, they would judge you, betray you, and they would leave you. You could give someone the world and be the most upstanding individual society had ever seen, you could even save someone's only child from a burning building, save *them* from a burning building, but the moment you slipped up or the moment you stood between them and their beliefs, even if by accident, you were dead to them. No matter how desperately you pleaded or how sincerely you explained, you were nothing to them. It wasn't because they hated you. It was because they didn't understand you. Really, it wasn't even that they didn't understand you. It was that they didn't understand themselves. They couldn't see their mistakes. They were blind to their own mania, partial to the darkness that stewed in their own hearts.

But Nate wasn't like that. He could understand others because, for better or worse, he understood himself. Today of all days, being in conversation with this sinister creature, he felt he understood himself more than he ever had. See, Nate knew and understood that he could stare into the face of a drunkard, of a cheat, of an addict, of a thief, of a murderer, and know that he was no better than they. Nate's deepest flaw above all else was his honesty.

So, Nate thought back to the rules that Ruth had told the group that morning. He wasn't sure he actually believed he'd be stuck here if the sun set while he was still inside the dark, but he equally wasn't sure he wanted to find out. How long had he been in here? How long had they been talking? By this point, it must have been hours, not an entire day, but many hours, which meant he'd need to get his answer quickly and be gone. He now understood the demon's game: to drag this out, to tell Nate what he really wanted to know only at the last possible moment. Then, Nate's mind drew back to the sun, the dying sun, sinking below the Earth to its temporary grave. The clock was ticking, faster and faster. The realization sent a heat wave through his skull and sweat down his spine.

Therefore, Nate was strategizing. He knew that if the demon could read his mind, he'd have to either distract it and trap it in its own ponder, or he'd have to think while the demon was speaking and then expel the thought the moment it finished and try to recollect the knowledge the instant it spoke next. He was doing this now and conceived it was the better of the two—

"Are you listening?" asked the demon patiently.

"Yes. I haven't gone deep enough."

"That's it, Nathan. Uncover the truth. It is the hidden emotion that is the true one, the one buried underneath, like a viper coiled in the brush, waiting to strike."

"Do you know what I'm going to do?"

"I am not the future, nor can I foresee it. I am a mirror."

"Then, you can't help me. You'll only reflect what I don't understand."

"Wrong. A mirror may not understand, but it also does not lie. A mirror is the only true path to full understanding. To look oneself in the eye is to unlock the potential of your reality. Do you understand?"

"The dark doesn't help you see, though. It prevents you from seeing."

"We must confront darkness to understand the fullness of being. Most of our universe is unknown, most lies in shadows."

"Am I trapped here? Am I your prisoner?"

"No. You are free to leave at any time you choose. In fact, it is I who is the prisoner."

"I'm afraid that I won't be able to leave here."

"I am not the source of your fears. You are."

"Earlier, you talked about me being a man of God. What's that got to do with what we're discussing here?"

"Everything. We either believe there is a God, or we believe we are God. God exists regardless."

"My faith is my greatest obstacle."

"Your faith is your greatest gift, or some might say."

"Why do I suddenly reject my faith that I once trusted undoubtedly? I tried to trust God. I tried to have faith."

"You left it behind."

"I didn't want to."

"You did. You always have."

"That's not true."

"Like I said. I cannot lie, Nathan."

"And I should trust you?"

"Would you trust yourself?"

"I gave everything to God. I followed him with every inch of my heart. I wasn't perfect, but when I finished serving, when I finished worship, I had so little left to give. I ran out of gas. I lost God. I lost my faith. And it was my faith that drove me away from it. I served God with everything, and that's the reason I have nothing."

"It is God's fault that your life is not perfect?"

"Isn't it? I was meant for something more. He put that on me."

"That is why you are here. You think I can show you. You think I can tell you."

"You can."

"That is right, Nathan. And only I can. But I do not think you can accept it. You will have to die to live. You will have to kill to save. You will have to sacrifice to gain. It is the only way."

"The only way for what?"

"To become who you are supposed to be.

"Who am I supposed to be?"

"Think, Nathan. Think."

"I don't know! Tell me!" Nate yelled.

"I cannot! It cannot be told. It must be perceived. Think about where we are. Think about who I am. You think I need you. You think I cannot leave this place without you. But you see, I can *only* leave this place without you."

"No. No. It can't be me."

"Do you believe the Lord can call you to do any-thing?"

"Yes."

"Anything?"

"Yes."

"Even *evil*?"

Nate stared deep into the bottomless yellow pits that were the demon's eyes, and Nate's own sprang wide with blood stripes. *It can't be*, Nate thought. *Not me.*

"Yes, Nathan. *You*. Did you not believe you were destined for greatness? Did you not believe you were chosen? Do you feel you have the right to question fate?"

"You're not asking me to do evil. You're asking me to become evil. To be the harbinger of everything corrupt and cruel. I don't accept," said Nate.

"But you know now. Therefore, you must. You see, you and I are not so different."

"We are nothing alike."

"I have come to serve you. I have come to lead your troops. I have come to advise you."

"I only take advice from God."

"God has led you here!" thundered the demon.

"He wouldn't do that. I led me here."

"He wouldn't do that, no. No, no, no. But he would leave His son to die. Is that it? If you do not accept, then you further disobey a God and a life

90

you've rejected. How far will you push Him? You're a leader, Nathan. You are THE leader. You are great. Who else could he send?"

"You."

"He will. Through you."

"I won't accept! I can still choose."

"Is that so? And tell me, Nathan. Did you really choose to come here? If you did, then you know I am correct. If you did not, then God is right. Which is it?" the demon hissed. His tongue slithered and crackled. His throat burned and steamed like an iron press.

The words dove into Nate's chest. What now was his way out? What was his strategy? The demon was much smarter than him and at this exact instant was registering every idea that came to him and all that would come. Nate knew, somehow, he knew, the moment he'd stepped in this room, he was trapped.

8

Their breath ran as quickly as their feet, snapping twigs and crunching brush within the darkening southern landscape. Summer and evening were always a strange mix in the South, strange yet ethereal. The creamsicle sky slept on the trees. The night air was lighter than the day, though not particularly cool. It smelled of honey and shaded green on the inconspicuous wind. The sunlit forest felt heaven-like because of its angelic glow. The flashing yellow bulbs of the fireflies matched the streaks in the clouds. It was amazing that something so delicate and so quiet sat so near the obscurity of the night. It was intentional. The proximity of the beast of the eve to the setting sun and its fleetingness was what made it so beautiful. It was as though squandering and limiting a thing were a necessity for the appreciation of it.

Ruth did her best to navigate their return at this rapid pace. Daphne was regaining strength but still unable to support her own weight. Amir's shoulder took the brunt of her and would soon need his own shoulder to rely on as his exhaustion intensified.

"Come on, Ruth. What'd you see in there?" said Amir.

Ruth kept moving faster.

"Why don't we just go to the police?" said Amir.

"They wouldn't believe us for a second."

"They might if we said someone needed help. They'd probably be curious enough anyway after we told them we'd found the house."

"They definitely wouldn't come if we told them we found the house. Even if the police came, there's no guarantee they'd get there in time. And if they don't get there in time, they'll think we played a prank or something, that we intentionally deceived them. I think this guy might be our best bet."

"This guy is a myth."

"So was that place."

"Is it true?"

"Is what true?"

"What they say about him, about the Unravel-er…"

"How he's the only person who's been to the house more than once?"

"Yeah."

"From what I've heard, yes, it's true."

"Has he been in *the dark* more than once?"

"Considering the state Daphne's in, if he has, he probably hasn't been more than twice."

"Where does he live?"

"Closer than the station."

"Would you be mad if I sent the police behind you? Just in case," said Amir with a crumpled wink.

"Only if you tell them that it was all your idea to come out here," replied Ruth.

"But it wasn't. And it wasn't yours either."

Ruth shrugged.

"I know you're adventurous, Ruth."

"And crazy," muttered Daphne.

"And crazy," Amir confirmed, "But not crazy enough to come out here. You would only do that for Nate."

"Olivia did it too," said Ruth.

"I think we all would for Nate, for one thing or another. How did he know where to go?"

"I don't know."

Resting for a moment, Amir offered Daphne to Ruth, who took her willingly. Amir leaned back into a tree and placed his hands on his knees, breathing in massive churns like the engine of an ocean liner. Their spare bottles had no more water, and the only fluid remaining in their bodies streamed from their pores in hot sweat. It coated their faces like wet wax and snuck between their hardening lips. The saltiness was sustenance in these conditions. It tasted cruel, but it tasted satisfying.

"Tell me what you saw in there," said Amir through his wheezing.

Ruth merely stared into the desolate, darkening forest that appeared as though it was slowly flooding with ink. The sherbet clouds continued shrinking on the horizon.

"I'm sorry, Amir, but we need to keep moving," said Ruth.

"Okay, up ahead at the break where the trees clear, we split. Hold her till then. I'll get Daphne to the hospital. You go and find this guy and get Nate and Olivia out of there."

They reached the break. Daphne made the switch back to Amir. Ruth turned to be on her way when Amir said—

"Ruth."

"I didn't see anything, but I heard something."

"What?"

"It sounded like Nate's voice, but it was older and heavier. In a way, it didn't sound like him at all."

"What did it say? I mean, what did *he* say?"

"He said, 'I will bring great destruction on the Earth.' But he spoke with such conviction. How could it be his voice? He wasn't in there yet."

"Maybe he's been before. Maybe that's how he knew where to go."

"Maybe."

"Ruth."

Ruth's twinkling, frightened eyes looked back into Amir's." Do you think Nate would hurt anyone?"

9

As the trees broke, Ruth slowed her sprint. She caught sight of the home on the other side of the field road. Smoke rolled from the chimney in black ribbons. The ribbons rose and cut into the orange clouds like cream. The evening shade clasped around squared windows that threw a red glow on the dirt lawn.

Ruth kept along the woven wire fence that led up to the yard. The home stood ahead like an omen. On either side of the drive were evenly spaced trees, each about fifteen or twenty feet tall, that stretched into the hills. Ruth plucked a piece of fruit from one of the trees nearest her. It was dark red and ovular. She crushed it in her palm. Between the broken skin and runny pulp was a peanut-like seed. The juice dribbled over the ridges of her skin and ran down her wrist. It was a cherry farm with a storehouse that sat back on the acreage.

As she neared the home, she saw the brick was beige and the door was black. She eased forward with noticeable trepidation. She inched into the red light the windows were casting and rose on her toes for a view inside. Suddenly, the black door shot open with a whap, the rusty hinges screaming. The fist that kept them at bay belonged to a shadow—formidable, God-like. The shadow was silhouetted against the red smolder, now pouring heavily into the night. Behind the silhouette, Ruth saw the source of the mysterious radiance. It was a crock fire on the hearth. But oddly, the flames were unfamiliar. They were not orange or yellow. They were red—deep red—the same as the cherries in the field. A glass of juiced cherries perched on a walnut cricket table, that, in the dim light, could rightly be mistaken for blood.

"Won't you come in?" the shadow said.

"Actually—" started Ruth.

"There's still time," said the shadow as it curled its bearded neck up to the burnt sky.

"Do you remember?" asked the demon when it already knew he did.

Nate dug deeper into his childhood. He never realized how much he resented doing this. He wasn't overly fond of his past, but he didn't think he hated it. But the more the demon pushed, the more he became spiteful of it. The more he analyzed, the more he understood, even a child, perhaps, especially a child, no matter their degree of innocence, could be vile.

Nate's mind rushed to second grade. Recess. The sun stood high overhead in the fall afternoon. The air was chilled, and the wind rolled across the skin like a whip. Nate's mouth was dry. His tongue stuck to the roof of his mouth and stung a little when it came back down. He was waiting in line for the monkey bars. He would usually spend most, if not all, of recess on them. He loved the cold snap that the cylindrical blue metal drove into his withered hands, parched from the autumn wind.

Refraining from inadvertent swaying was the key to maintaining leverage and making it across the gap to the other side of the jungle gym some twenty feet away. Nate knew this, but at present, a boy blocked his path and the continuation of a decent recess. Nate couldn't remember his name, but he did remember that the boy was afraid. He was a little too short to reach the first bar and would have to make a jump to catch it. It was a jump the boy was not looking forward to making. Growing heavily impatient, Nate didn't ask the boy if he could go first. He didn't even tell him to get a move on. He merely pushed the boy off the ledge to the crumbled rubber bed below. The bed of the playground wasn't exactly cement, but it wasn't a mattress either. The boy, for some reason, pitched face forward. His nose connected square with one of the large supporting poles of the playground with a *clang*. Nate later found out that his nose was indeed broken. The boy blacked out. He didn't know who pushed him and never would.

Nate scanned his immediate surroundings. Somehow, he was fortunate enough that no students or teachers were in a close enough vicinity of the monkey bars to have witnessed the crime. Nate didn't know why he did it. Where did the impulse come from, and why so suddenly, and why was it so seemingly uncontrollable? Was it from some hidden force buried within himself that he'd yet to unlock? Was it some genetic predisposition passed down from the branches of his family tree? Was it his parents and their overbearingness and their secret apathy that he so desperately resented? If it was resentment for his parents, he wondered why it chose to express itself in such an odd manner. He wondered if it'd happen again, and if, like before, he'd be unable to control the inclination.

He could hardly remember he'd even done it, but the act sent a bolt of pain into his skull. His eyelids flexed, and his brain clenched. For a moment, it felt like he'd been pushed and smacked the metal pole with his face. He'd felt the blood on his lip and the taste of iron on his tongue. The thought hurt

Nate's soul and crushed it slightly. He held back from exploding into tears.

"So, you see, you are capable of it," said the demon.

"Anyone is. I already knew that," said Nate.

"There is sin, and then, there is evil."

"You're saying I never knew innocence."

"I am saying, most children do have both innocence and impurity in them to varying degrees. You, however, only had one."

"I didn't have control then."

"You always wanted to be on top."

"You think I don't have control, but I don't have to give in to you."

"You do not have to give in, but you will. You can't suppress this forever. Sooner or later, it will leak out. In fact, the more you suppress, the bigger the bubble grows. It is only a matter of time before it pops. The suppression feeds the desire, not the indulgence of it. Feeding a wild creature puts it to sleep. Withholding the meal only riles it up, only sharpens its focus, makes it keener to obtain the thing which it so desires."

"I want to be great."

"You are too afraid to be great."

"I don't deserve to be great."

"That is still fear."

"I thought I was supposed to be afraid. But now I'm not so I can serve the Lord?"

"That's right."

"I need fear to serve Him, but I also need to eliminate fear to serve Him."

"Yes. You see the contradiction in His nature."

"Or the contradiction in your theory."

"You are afraid to accept the truth."

"So what if I am?"

"The question is simple. Is fear good or is it bad? Is living in fear a good thing? If it is good, then God is great. If it is bad, then you are free to go your own way."

"I think fear can be healthy."

"Why?"

"It keeps us cautious."

"Caution makes you weak."

"It makes you focused."

"If it did, then you wouldn't be here."

"Why did I do it?" Nate asked with a sudden quiver.

"Because it is who you are, who you *really* are."

"You want me to start a war?"

"Yes."

"How?"

"Not with force. At least, not yet. You belong with the damned, Nathan. That is your calling. That is how you can ultimately and fully serve the Lord and fulfill your purpose."

"I don't believe you, but I don't believe myself either. I've tried so hard to be perfect and follow every rule. There's so much I've missed out on."

"You missed out because you were afraid to do those things."

"There's that word again."

"That is right, Nathan. Fear is God. Fear is who you serve. And as long as you bow before it, you will never see what you truly are, what you truly could be. You must admit that you are wrong. You must admit that you are weak. You must admit that God and the world owe you nothing, and yet somehow, you ask for everything. Now, repeat after me: I am not a good person."

The red blaze kicked shadows across the wall that danced between the cracks of the faded striped wall-paper. Ruth watched them sway, as she'd yet to muster the courage to make the shadow's acquaintance. Rather, she gulped her third helping of cherry juice. The curvature of the wine glass fit perfectly to her weathered lips. Tilting it toward the ceiling as she drank, the sweet nectar slipped down her cheek and then her neck. The shadow watched it slide with a hungry curiosity, then drank its own glass of blood-red juice.

Ruth again tried to converse, "We need to—"

"There is time. Talk some with me, and I'll tell ya how to save yer friend."

They sat there another minute or two, but it seemed like hours. Ruth began to squirm in her seat, adjusting her back and then fidgeting her legs and twisting her shoulders. She was balled up and tense. The shadow remained relaxed, sitting in its ladderback rocker that spat out ghoulish whispers with each creak. The room smelled old and tart. The old most likely came from the colonial plaster walls, which molded in the corners, the tart from the pails brimmed with cherries. All was strange but calm until the shadow leaned into the red glow of the fire. The shadow became a man, half of his face covered in darkness, the other coated in blood light. His eyes bulged and cracked and flooded with branching vessels. Ruth's neck lurched backward as her throat tightened and closed. She swallowed hard at what was before her. The man looked to be some two hundred years old, if not more. His cheeks were draped in folds like curtains. His eyelids hung sideways, and his forehead was a series of heavy lumps.

"Never taste fruit quite like that, have ya?" said the Unraveler. "What's it taste like to ya?"

"Tastes like life," whispered Ruth.

"How's life taste?"

"Fresh. Full. Rich."

"Takes a good long time for fruit to ripen. Once it's ready, only got so long to eat it before it turns to rot. That's life," said the scabbed man.

"How do I get him out of the dark?" She said this as she absorbed just how grim the house was. The curvy red flames and the glass containers reflecting them were the only light there was.

"Ya mean, how's he see the light again? Can ya even see the light once ya seen the dark?"

"Can you?"

"S'pose that depend on the individual. Haw-ever, if a person can change, I s'pose they could change back."

"What if they never really changed in the first place? What if they just discovered who they really were? What if there is no change? What if we're all just constant?"

"Or constantly changin'."

"You don't believe in change. I can see it."

A cheeky and corrupt smile snuck across his lower face. "I believe in real-ization." The man's teeth were bronze with decay. Saliva slithered between the crooked gaps. "I believe once a man know more than he ought, he ought to know no more. If ya pick my drift. Or rather he hopes."

"The truth shouldn't always remain hidden."

"Sometimes it should. Once a man know his destiny, he's destined to undo it. The opposite, the ironic, will always be the stronger vice. Ta tell a man his destiny is ta prove that he got no grip over his reality."

"Presenting someone with a fact isn't the same as forcing them to accept it."

"I never heard of someone refutin' a fact. That'd make it *not* a fact."

"Then, there is no fact. There is no absolute."

"Jus' cus ya can't accept it, don't mean ya can refuse it." The glittering blaze in the fireplace popped and crackled, as if reinforcing the man's speech, as if promoting it.

"They say you've been there, to *the dark*, and come back."

The man leaned forward even closer to Ruth, so close that she tucked her chin and bent her head back and to the side. She could smell the tobacco in his gums and the odor of the garlic-dredged liverwurst he'd had for dinner. His eyes gleamed like a famished grizzly in the red half-light. "What makes ya think I ever left?"

10

Blue neon EKG lines streamed in a steady zag. Saline dripped in drops intravenously into Daphne's right cephalic vein. The upper half of her body rested at a slight incline in the hospital bed. Her eyelids eased open and closed and opened again against the blaring fluorescent bulbs. The room smelled flat and metallic. The air felt like the inside of a refrigerator that shot waves of mountainous goosebumps up Daphne's arms. Daphne cranked her head toward Amir's, which hung on his left shoulder as he slouched asleep in the chair beside the bed. The infrequent beeps of medical machines, the rustling papers of patient chartings, and the squeaks of poorly greased wheelchairs drifted in from the hallway and swelled into a strange medley of unpleasant sounds.

Daphne's gaze rolled about the room for a minute or so. Then, Amir came to.

"Did you call the cops?" Daphne's voice sounded rusted over.

"Ruth didn't want me to, remember? She always has things under control," said Amir.

"Or she thinks she does."

They shared an easy laugh and a frank stare that followed it that said: We should do this more often, just the two of us. Despite the strange dynamic of the group, the five friends were practically inseparable and would do nearly everything together. Whether it be a movie or a football game and tailgate or even heading to the dry cleaners, for some reason, they felt the need to do it as one rather than as individuals. It gave them a sense of power, a sense of connection, a sense of life. Nothing could compare to the early summer evening drives where the A/C was broken, the windows were low, and the car speaker shouted along with them as they yelped in half-harmony to some soothing radio hit. Time stretched out on the open road before them. The low country rising in the heat. Longleaf pines, southern magnolias, bald cypresses, and palmettos stood steady and unshakable in the distance, as if eternity was resting a moment in their shade, as if perpetuity was all the day had to offer. Then the trees fled by, and the sunset melted into the stars.

"I wanted to make sure you were okay," Amir assured her.

Trying to shake the mucus in her lungs, Daphne said, "What do you care?"

"Why else would I be here?"

"You should get the police."

"Why?"

Daphne choked and coughed and spat phlegm into a cup. Her voice came and went, came and went. She stretched again for speech, "He should…" and she lost it.

"Take it easy. Nate's going to come out. They'll be fine. We'll all be fine. Maybe this *Unraveler* will go get him, or maybe Ruth will pull something off."

"Police… Police…"

"—aren't going to help Nate. There's no point in bothering."

Daphne was shaking her head fiercely. She desperately wanted to spit out words rather than flecks. She desperately wanted to say something more, something that her fierce grip, strangling Amir's arm, showed was deeply important.

The red fire was bone-thin and soon going down for a nap. Red juice in jars and other oddly shaped glasses and the metal buckets of fresh, burgundy cherries shot baroque shadows on the striped walls and made the room appear more hellish than ever. Ruth couldn't stop swallowing or knotting her fingers between one another. Her glance kept snapping to the window and the inches of day left in the sky.

The Unraveler was reclining again in his rocker. The grooves of its laddered back sunk into the rolls of his heavy skin. The crying red shadows from the blaze waltzed on the drooping flabs of his face. A sparse flicker lit up his eyes, which flooded with vessels and were savage-like. The dim smolder in combination with the pointed ears on the cresting rail of the man's chair made him appear like a multi-faceted beast.

"How do you get back to the house if you've already been? I know you're the only one who knows."

"There is no house." Outside the window, lightning cracked. The bold, jagged streak looked red through the cherry jars. The lightning was alone. The sky was empty of any possible storm. The flash came from nothing. "Strange," he croaked.

"You said you would help me."

The man arched his neck back, squeezing the creases in the skin. He acknowledged the state of the sun's position. "I save about all I could save. That being, them whom I could save. But them whom I could save didn't really need me to save 'em, if ya catch my meanin'. I tell ya the truth. I been to the house and come back. I been to the dark and come back. I seen about everythin' a man can see. But even I ain't ever seen nobody last this long."

"You're saying he'll never come out."

"I'm sayin' he will, but you gon' wish he hadn't."

"You were never going to help me?"

"Nobody can help you. Nobody ever could. Fate has come for yer friend. He's come for all of ya. That sun gon' set, and it gon' be a long time 'for it ever come back up." A laugh split the room like dark thunder. It was a vile, wicked cackle. It roared from the man in the shadows, whose chest heaved and sank in ripples. Ruth stood carefully and sidestepped toward the door, carefully easing past the man with trembling feet. She blasted through the screen door and vaulted the porch. As she sped back down the dusty drive and the rows of cherry trees surrounding it, she could hear that unceasing and terrible cackle drifting behind her with the dust clouds.

Daphne continued to scratch for speech while Amir tried his best to calm her. Her neck was raised off the bed and tilted towards him. He leaned forward and pressed her shoulders back down toward the bed. Daphne shook slightly, her teeth protruding from her mouth with saliva hanging on the edges.

"Police… Police…" again she croaked.

"What's wrong? You want me to get the police? Okay. I'll get the police and send them out there. It's not a big deal."

Now, her hand shot out like a crab's pincer. Daphne's fist was curling inward, twisting the sleeve of Amir's shirt. "I… remember…" she said, but Amir couldn't quite hear.

He leaned forward further with his hands on the bed rails. His palms squeezed the hard plastic with increasing intensity. His head arched forward on his neck like a desk lamp. Daphne's claws were pulling him toward her. It would have seemed to be for a kiss if not for the crooked expression on Daphne's face, her eyebrows tilting inward and downward, and the glabella between them rumpling together in terror.

"Amir…"

"What? What? I'm here. I'm right here! What is it?"

"Nate…"

"What about Nate? I'll send help. If you'll let go, I'll call the police right now."

"Don't." Her voice snapped back with frightening crispness and clarity.

"What?" Amir asked, perplexed.

"I remember what I saw in that place. In… *the dark*."

"You came out laughing."

"I was laughing because that's how I cope with things that horrify me. I laugh at horror movies not because I think they're funny but because they scare me to death. I was laughing because it was all too real."

"What did you see?"

"I can't repeat it. I don't ever want to repeat it."

"Why don't you want me to send the police?"

"You can send the police. You can send whoever you want, but only to stop Nate."

"I don't understand."

"Amir…"

"What, Daph? What!" His voice kept rising in irritation. Nurses shot glances from the desk down the hall. Some patients turned their heads, too. Even the fluorescent lights in the ceiling stretched brighter and were prepared to punch out of the glass prisons of their bulbs. The room felt as though it was closing inward.

"I don't think Nate should leave the room. I don't think he should be… _let out_." Daphne collapsed back onto the bed in frailty and deep heaves. The EKG spat out strange curves and low-toned groans. Nurses soon swarmed the room. The fluorescent lights screamed brighter. The chill grew colder and heavier.

Amir began to scoot back from Daphne as though she had suddenly contracted some highly contagious disease. His eyelids were dams holding back tears on the verge of breaking hard. Despite the chaos that now crowded the room, one thing remained the same: Daphne's deep gaze, crazed and horrified, stabbing into Amir's, feeling the same.

11

Those glaring yellow cat eyes with the feral black dots in the centers still fastened to the darkness, but they were sharper now. They tilted more at an angle, as if growing weary or angry. Nate couldn't stand to look at them another second, but at the same time, couldn't look away. The room was cold now and smelled of death. Nate had hunted with his father before. He remembered the smell of a rotting carcass and of a burning one, too. This was worse. He didn't bother to speak up about it because he knew the demon had already heard what he was thinking. Nate wondered why it was so difficult for him to do the same to the demon. The demon had some impenetrable defense mechanism, some unbreachable mental wall in place. The demon trained its mind to be unbreakable. Nate hoped perhaps this place could help him do the same.

They both still stood in the same positions opposite one another in the room. Nate was spent, but even though they'd been standing in the same position for hours, his legs didn't feel tired or weak. In fact, he could hardly feel them at all. Nate's mind continued to creep back to that day at the playground.

"Why did I do it?"

"You mean, the boy?" said the demon.

"He did nothing wrong."

"Well, I suppose not at that time, but we all will grow to do wrong things. We all are the demons we so desperately despise. But most fail to look as inward as you, Nathan."

"I feel this unbearable weight on my chest all the time, and it's bending my will to keep going. It's choking my heart. It's drying up my bones. No matter what I pray, God won't take it away. My idols won't either."

"Your heroes."

"I suppose they did for a time. They gave me peace and inspiration."

"Your idols will destroy you."

"Why?

"Because they are as hollow as you have been."

"Are you an idol?"

The demon laughed. It was a coarse laugh. It was a cruel laugh, and it echoed and clanged in Nate's ears. "Do you still not know me, Nathan?"

"And my friends…"

"Your friends are and will always be in a different place than you. They will tell you they are there for you, but they will never really be there. They cannot relate to you, and you cannot relate to them."

"Why not?"

"We are all destined for something, but most of us will never see it and see the pain required to reach it."

"I've always felt I was close to death."

"Very close. Death gives you life. It is not as people think. The closer you are, the stronger you get. Most people are too alive to live."

"Wha—"

"They are machines, Nathan, with the inability to think, but not you. It's time to accept the truth of who you really are."

"What truth?"

"You are no different from me."

"I'll go in myself if I have to," Ruth said to herself as she raced between the wide oaks heavy with Spanish moss. The last of the sunset cut between the curves in the bark. The day had only moments left, and somehow, this sun felt final. It was a heavy sun that felt as though it was bringing the world down with it. It was a swallowing sun. Ruth caught this end of day in the corner of her eye and dug her feet harder into the dirt. Ruth had been runner-up in the varsity cross country state championship for AAA. She did it because she loved it and the social aspect of it. One never understood how things like that could come in handy until they did. Ruth ran and ran and ran until a row of stabbing, diamond-twisted finials broke the coils in the trees. It was the top of the black gate, and it jabbed skyward in the coming distance.

"Where is God in this moment?"

"I cannot lie, Nathan. He is here. He is always here. He is everywhere," said the demon.

They raised their voices now. They were no longer speaking in their heads, but they were audibly speaking, shouting.

"Then, why do I not feel him? Why do I not believe he's there if I know he's there?"

"You still do not see it. You still do not see why you have really come here."

"Why?"

"You are utterly and completely alone. It is what's tearing you apart. It is what's destroying you. Even God recognized that man cannot be alone. There are things even *He* cannot do. That is why he created Eve. You either need to let God take your pain and your fears and your struggles, or you need to give them over to Him. Either way, it is your responsibility. Once again, either way, you are alone. Isn't that funny?"

But Nate wasn't laughing. The weight of the truth in the demon's words was practically unbearable. In his heart, Nate knew, he knew it was true. What now was his escape? What now was his way out? He possessed nothing but surrender. Finally, he erupted—

"All right, I'm alone! I'm alone! What does it matter? What does it mean?"

"It means you are free. Only the lonely are free. Only the lonely can see. Only the lonely can change. Only the lonely can become!"

"Become what?!" yelled Nate with terrible scratches in his throat.

"*ANYTHING!*" the demon thundered.

Day's last sliver of life slanted across the attic floor and the far wall. The light angled upward at the crux in the floor's break. It was rising on that shadowed door, that gateway to Hell. The entryway swallowed the light whole. The position of the door was perfect east in that it would be the last thing the light would see. The sun was low and hit the bars on the pane in such a way that the cross silhouette it reflected was tall and mighty. It cut directly across the black doorway and stretched over most of the wall. It was a foreboding sight. Olivia only acknowledged the strangeness of it, as her head came down from savoring the last of the second water bottle.

Her eyes were low, and the bags under them were lower. Her lips were dry and ached with crust. She took in air in long, arduous boatloads. Olivia eyed the third and last bottle lounging on the floor by the window. She leered at it, then trudged over, reaching for it. Her palm hovered and then retracted into a fist. Her gaze tilted up to the low, yellow gash drowning in the darkening sky, about to dip below the horizon. Her watch read 8:40 PM—three minutes from sunset. She turned slowly toward the dark, rectangular void with its fiendish trim. She took a reluctant step in its direction, then another, then another. Her hands broke into a tremor, and her ankles quivered, as she drew nearer to the all-con-suming dark.

"Nate," she mustered.

The darkness was heavy, and to Nate, the room felt as if it was spinning in a thousand different circles. His thoughts began to cluster and spiral, each stick-ing and then detaching from the other, unable to form a chain or semblance. Escape was past him. This was about survival. He again pondered the demon's true intentions and the nature of its words. There lay a hint of encouragement in them. If the demon believed Nate was unstoppable, why did it appear to have every intention of getting in his way? It felt as though the demon was getting smarter and Nate less so.

Nate bled for an idea, a strategy, but the notion completely alluded him. He was feeling it now, the heat of reality, the exhaustion of this unwholesome day, this living nightmare. He had nothing and knew sunset drew near. He didn't know just how close it was or that he even believed in Ruth's silly rules, but after being in this place, this *dark*, he knew, if it were possible, he'd do anything to get out. Nate had the sudden urge to move, and the demon raised an eyebrow.

"You are sick, Nathan. You are very sick. But no one knows just how sick you really are. Not even you," said the demon. In his heart, Nate knew it was true.

Nate admitted, "I feel like I'm on the verge of total mental collapse—"

"—and when I break, I don't know what's going to happen." The demon stole the words from Nate's head before he could even utter them.

It spooked Nate deeply. He knew the demon could read his mind, but how could it think of something he hadn't even thought of yet? Fear grew in

Nate's chest like a fungus, like a bacterium that no medicine could treat.

"You want me to carry this out, but I feel like I'm dying."

"A star burns brightest at its end. And your end and its beginning have come."

"The world will bleed with or without me."

"That is where you are wrong. Without you, without us, the world will never die. It will go on believing it is alive. I tried to save you. I tried to show you. I tried to guide you. I was prepared to hold your hand through the blasting inferno. Now, Nathan, I have a task to carry forth from *my* God, and since you have no respect for yours, I must do it alone. I must do it myself. If you do not control what frightens you, Nathan, it will control you. As a matter of fact, it already does."

At that moment, for the first time, the demon took a step closer toward Nate. It was a booming thud that agitated the ground. The heel hit like a boot, and the toes like claws. The step fired a bolt of fear down

Nate's spine, such as he'd never felt before, and he prayed he'd never feel again.

"You feel it, don't you? You dug into flesh and muscle, and now you finally see the bone. Is it white like you've been taught? Or is it as black as death?" said Nate. His face contorted and coiled and scrunched. *Did those words just come from me?*

I need to leave. I need to leave now, thought the demon, and closer it stepped.

I need to get out, Nate thought. *I need to be great*, he thought again. *If I'm stuck here in the darkness, I'll never be anything.*

Closer, the demon stepped. Fear roped around Nate and pulled tight.

I need to accept what I'm here to do, thought the demon.

Closer, it stepped.

I need to embrace what only I was called to do, thought Nate.

Closer.

Step aside, Nathan, thought the demon.

Closer. Nate felt the vibrations from the demon's stomp rattle his shins.

I know my calling, thought Nate, *I know to get where I'm going, I must destroy you!*

CLOSER.

The only thing you need to destroy is yourself. We must all do that to confront our fate, to own it, but you could not. You squandered your potential when you had so much to give. Only you saw the truth, thought the demon. *Only you knew—*

The family of a murdered daughter will offer no forgiveness for her killer. Their anger blinds them from the knife they themselves are holding, and the murder they will soon commit against the daughter of another, thought Nate.

We're all killers, thought the demon.

Through and through, thought Nate.

We're all capable of it. That is what makes us the same. If you can love a killer, if you can take him into your heart, you will become the truth, you will become the life, thought the demon. *You understand, now accept. It is I, Nathan, I who will rule!*

"NOW, BOW!" said the demon with a roar.

CLOSER IT STEPPED!

I WON'T! Thought Nate.

CLOSER!!!

BOW! Thought the wicked creature.

I FEEL IT, thought Nate.

"What is it you feel?" it said, with a smile of absolute malice.

"What you're thinking. I know the answer now. I know the way to get the weight off my chest. I know what you've been hiding. In coming into my thoughts, you've let me into your own. I know what it means to have innocence."

"And what is that?" said the demon.

"Control," said Nate, and he burst for the exit.

12

Light surged back into Nate's squinting eyes like an oncoming car on a night road. The attic wasn't bright, but it wasn't anywhere near the pitch black of where he'd just been. For a split second, as he shot out of the dark, his eyes were so dilated that each iris was almost completely covered by the pupil, making his eyes look black and unholy. They began to constrict as the starlit attic emerged into hazy view with its fungus-painted walls and swamp-puddled floorboards.

Olivia was stepping inside the dark, and every muscle she had tensed as Nate barreled out of it. Not expecting her, Nate sacked Olivia, and they clattered to the attic floor with a splash and a bang, somersaulting across the room. Olivia's glasses tumbled off and rolled into a puddle.

For a split second, Nate lay on her, partly paralyzed in amazement at the face of another human being and partly in wonderment that he had someone in his life who cared enough to wait around for him in a tomb like this. Somehow, he knew it would be her there waiting for him. It would be Olivia.

Olivia matched his expression with an aghast one of her own. Nate's face was so worn it practically blended with the shredded walls. His face melted with sweat, which was dripping onto hers. His under eyes were purpled and saggy. Marks of soot streaked his forehead and upper cheeks. His lips were white and brittle, his breath odorous and hot. Heat radiated from his skin like an overused engine. Olivia's shock simmered and rested. Gazing into her eyes, hers back into his, a smile worked its way across Nate's grim teeth. Then reality sprang back in a flash. Nate shot up, yanking Olivia by the arm. He scrambled for the spiral staircase. Olivia broke his grip to recover her glasses from the murky puddle. Nate reached back and yanked her again.

"Run, Olivia! Run!" he screamed.

Olivia glanced back as Nate dragged her toward the stairwell. Just as they were going down, a pair of wicked claws wrapped around the outside of the entrance to the dark. They gripped the outer frame and crumpled the depraved molding with dust dreaming of the indentations. As Nate and Olivia spun down the steps, right before the doorway fled from Olivia's sight, two horrible, ravenous yellow eyes stabbed out of the blackness.

Olivia and Nate found themselves back in the elongated upstairs hallway. It was eerily dark, and only sparse moonlight gave the dinginess character. The hallway stretched and stretched, so far that the end of it wasn't in sight, but they ran as if it was. Bolting down the wide expanse at maximum speed, Nate filed through thoughts and ideas to think of an escape, to think of the way they came, but he couldn't. His mind was shooting blanks. Racing at full tilt, they both stole a look back in the direction of the red velvet staircase that led to the third floor. There—tall and straight and menacing—was the demon. Its shaded, leathery skin stood distinct against the velvet. It was out, and its fiendish teeth and razor claws had no intention of resting until Nate and Olivia were locked inside them.

Before the pair could fully pivot their heads back around—SLAM! A blockade of plaster pummeled them backward. Olivia's glasses cracked against the wall as her head bashed into it and again as she smacked the floor. Nate's shoulder cracked and popped against the barricade that looked as if it had been there the entire time, as if that's how the house was built. It was a dead end that cut off the rest of the corridor and appeared from nowhere. But Nate knew, he knew now the demon was doing some thinking of its own. It controlled the house as much as Nate had when they arrived. He could alter the architecture in a moment, the same way Nate found entrance to the dark.

The demon eased toward them, its toes digging into the hardwood. It held its arms steady and calm at its sides as it glided down the passageway. Rare moonlight glittered off its metallic talons that danced in an excited rhythm. As it drew near, tears slipped below the cracked glass of Olivia's spectacles. Nate plowed into his thoughts, his mind racing for the exit to the hallway. Deeper and further he dug, but he only found emptiness. There was no way out. He couldn't outthink the demon any more than a hanging man could outthink a noose. And the demon—with its sly grin and sharp eyes—knew it. The house was a coffin ready to open, with the demon ready to throw Nate and Olivia in it.

A soft lunar spotlight beamed down between the trees from the dark blue sky above. The sky was deep and rich. The coming moon reflected off shiny badges stitched to polyester, stars glimmering in the gold. Amir considered the heavy sky with unease. He marched forward with the cops trailing behind him. There were five of them. Most were deputies who were on their way out the door when Amir had arrived at the station in a panic. The sheriff had to take the lead, whether he wanted to or not.

He was more concerned with happy parents than a good night's rest. He knew—as he'd told his men—an unhappy parent is as much pain as a bullet, and with better aim, too. A missing kid didn't look good, but it would look even worse in the morning. So, the sheriff took Amir seriously, and so here they were.

Usually, with Amir's history of mischief, the cops would be called *on* Amir, not *by* him. The police were also half-interested in seeing if the house actually existed. Everyone knew about it. Most had never seen it.

Moving as a pack with Amir at the point, the forest seemed to stretch endlessly. The oaks seemed like a mouth ready to swallow them in darkness. The southern heat pushed sweat into the eyes and mouths of the men. The air smelled like fire. They breathed it in with heavier and heavier gasps. The pressure of the situation was nearly visible on Amir's worried brow that continued to sink with each plod. Amir's sweeping eyes made it apparent that he had no idea where he was leading them. Then a crackle broke the labored breathing and the cicadas, a snap in the thicket. It sounded like the crunching of bones. The group froze, and the sheriff's hand instinctively hovered toward his holstered belt pistol. Two figures miraged in the forlorn light, then only one. Then a pair of evil, yellow eyes opened and hung in the wooded blackness.

Nate's mind cleared despite the oncoming force of death swarming toward them.

Removing the wall that hindered them was Nate's only desperate thought. He pictured in his head that the way forward was open. Disintegrating that wall—for the moment—was all he was. In a flash, with the thought of freedom blasting out of his brain, Olivia and Nate registered that the blockage had evaporated, and passage was wide and free. As they began to run, Nate thought of every possible exit he could—doors, rooms, staircases that led to the lower levels. They appeared, but as soon as they did, the demon came up with something better—brick walls behind the doors, empty rooms, and more end-less passageways, stairwells to bottomless pits—the moment Nate thought of his offensive. The switch was almost instantaneous. It *was* instantaneous, as though Nate thought of the barricades himself. They became interchangeable, as though the demon was thinking of the exits and Nate was blocking them. It was a mind puzzle with Nate on his toes at every turn and the demon on his heels. Olivia was just along for the ride, but her analysis of Nate as she studied his face during the life-or-death mind race was as horrifying as the game the demon was playing.

Gravel crunched under Ruth's soles as she slid through the gate and churned down the long, straight drive. Looming at its end, the great home was crumbling, decaying in real time. Cracks split the stone in ragged jags. Dust drizzled from the chimneys rocking in place. For the moment, the support of the structure held. The fractures were merely surface-level, but some left breaches in between. There were slight holes, openings, in the limestone, through which someone could pass sideways. Ruth was already at the breaks and had the intention of doing just that. Going headfirst, she slipped into one of the mouths in the stone as new cracks formed and splintered in the sides of the fortress. The house was coming down sooner or later.

13

When she finally realized there was someone else in the room with her, the paralysis of her dreams was still wearing off slightly and throwing her vision into a blur. She saw two specs of red that could have been lights for a machine that a nurse had rolled into the room while she was sleeping. It was only after a minute or so, when the swimming of her mind began to calm, that the two fiery red eyes clung to reality and the still room, but these were not the eyes of some mythical dream creature. They were the eyes of a man, an old man, whose skin folded on itself and was so thick and heavy it looked like sacks of flour piled on each other. It was the Unraveler, and his meaty hands slumped on the footboard of Daphne's bed. The two stared at each other for some solid length of time.

He had large rings on his right hand that he tapped in waves against the hard plastic, making a drumming succession. The sound filled the room as it grew in volume. It grew louder and louder. Daphne's face tightened at the roll of the rings and leaned away as if dodging the sharp rays of the mid-afternoon sun. The continual patter was accompanied by a rotten smile that looked dead and forgotten. The rolling clatter of the gold rings ceased.

"You seen somethin' ya wasn't s'pose to see. Now, it's my job to clean it on up," said the Unraveler.

"So you decide what I see and don't see?" said Daphne, still weak in the bones.

"That ain't for you to know."

"But it's for me to accept, right?"

"That's right. We all capable of gaining sight but some a us are meant to stay blind."

"Who decides?"

"Not me." He coughed out a slick cackle that flickered the lights. "Ya may wanna ask yer friend, but here again, I believe ya already did."

"Nate isn't well."

"And you is?" he said with a nasty grin.

Daphne's body went rigid.

"You all belong in 'at place of death but ya think ya got a right to sit it out and judge. That dark as much yers as anybodys. I do believe it's especially yers."

The Unraveler's glance shifted toward something sitting on the silver medical table beside the bed. Daphne's head slowly creaked to follow. A syringe lay sweetly on the metal, and tears began to roll down her cheeks like a rainstorm on a windshield.

"So yer vision finally comin' to, but whatcha didn't realize is that the dark is the light. We is the worse parts of ourselves."

"I guess so."

"It's okay. Yer actions don' change nothin'. We are who we are. You was right to think it. But you was wrong ta think you any better." The Unraveler's dry mouth clapped in its stickiness. He brought a wine glass of sweet cherry juice to his lips that he had not been holding before. His Adam's apple jabbed outward with each lustful gulp. Daphne's face warped at the sight.

"Will the others be spared?" she said.

"Will you, ya mean?" said the Unraveler.

"I already know the answer to that since you're here. What about Ruth, Amir, Olivia?"

"It's funny, ain't it? Ya gotta be blind to see. They joined 'im. Should they not share his fate?"

"Not Olivia. I don't know if there was ever such a thing as innocence, but if there's even a drop of purity left on this earth, it's in her."

"She may had had more sight than the rest of ya, but she still too blind to see she in love with the devil."

The mind clash between Nate and the demon roared on. With each alteration to the mansion's formation, boards buckled, corroded plaster crinkled, and the floors began to crease and ditch into small, moldy trenches. The house was deteriorating under their reckless game of mental combat. They were disintegrating its teetering beauty and about to take themselves down in the process. The house was nearing its end. There was no stopping it.

The changes in architecture and structure became more elaborate—arch bridges of grinded elm and torn carpet, trapdoors to chasms of void, hollow rooms that were craters in time, staircases in the air. Nate was borderline asphyxiated under the strain of this cognitive warfare.

At another dead end lay an impenetrable barricade of illogical stone and brick, layers upon layers deep. The demon prowled closer, its starving talons sinking into the spoiled wood, its claws leaving sinuous braids in the plaster.

Corrupting the shadows, its yellow eyes were cosmic and striking. They were a burning match that would not be snuffed out willingly. Two circular cavities that were empty and vile broke the center of the yellow, and that stare that was more menacing than ever glided phantom-like between the rifts in the dust. The stare stabbed at Nate and Olivia's chests, splitting the breastbone.

The demon's seared figure sharpened at the shoulders as the edges of its skin spiraled in ornate construction. The limbs were pointed and lasting. Olivia wrapped her hand in Nate's and weaved her fingers into his. Their skin tightened together as if it were molded.

Nate turned to her, latched onto her gaze, and lost himself in it. Her eyes were as shattered as the cracked lenses they were looking through. Nate brought her close to him, as the demon stamped towards them, its clawed toes clattering in an anxious roll on the aged wood. It raised a hand outward, and its scythe-like fingernails burned for them.

A smile broke the sternness and fear on Nate's face. Olivia eased as well at the sight of it. Nate took a hand and wiped back the hair hanging over her glasses. "I'm sorry."

"I came here with you because I thought I wanted to stop you, but I just want to be with you, whichever *you* that is."

"When we try to be the wrong thing, Nathan, we are nothing at all," snapped the demon.

The sheriff and his deputies inched closer to the yellow discs screaming out from the wooded pit. Following his lead, each unlatched and raised their pistols at the demonic gaze resting in the deep, lying steady, patiently. Making an etched outline in the dense forest, the shimmering claws of what appeared to be the figure's hands shone like silver weapons. Sweat slipped down the palms of the men and between the grips of their guns, which were shaking at the sight of this shadow beast. The sheriff took his flashlight and rolled the beam of light up the dirt and the roots toward the figure, but the beam died several feet before it, as if it had been snipped off at the end, swallowed by the darkness so heavy light couldn't enter it.

In the back of the group, something unnatural latched onto the corner of Amir's eye and nestled there, pressing him to acknowledge it. As he twisted around, he was partially blinded by what looked like liquid jewels. They shone with a red gleam that worshipped the moonlight providing them their glitter. A wine glass encased the jewels. It tilted upward, and the sparkling liquid tumbled down the lumpy throat of a man leaning on an oak. His skin was so old and rough it nearly blended with the bark. He proffered the glistening glass toward Amir, beckoning him for a drink, for only a sip.

"You been racin' round all day, hows about you take a drink. You earned it," said the Unraveler.

"You're him, aren't you?" Amir asked softly.

The man hunched forward into the shaft of moonlight that carved the trees from above. The twinkling beam slid between the branches, spitting hellish barbs across his face. "Who?"

"Where's Ruth? Where's Nate? Did they get out?"

"Take ya a sip and I tell ya."

The man pulled some cherries from his grungy pocket. He crushed the fruit in his fist, mangling the pulp. The dense juice trickled down the flaps in his skin and bled into the glass. Amir glanced back toward the police, who were oblivious of this exchange, still laser-focused on that threatening, golden gaze and the shadow stilted with damnation that bore it.

"Oh, they can't help ya no more. They can't even help themselves."

"Do they see it?"

"See what?"

"The eyes."

"Whatever they do see, it'll be the last thing."

The sheriff and his trembling men inched closer to the bent shadow, their dread swelling. The toes of their boots dragged heavily, collecting dirt in the leather folds. Their heels hovered before easing back down to the weeds. Index fingers garnished with sweat held hot to the triggers.

Rooms shifted their form as Ruth sped from one to the other. The walls shook with such fierce force that the lath in the ceiling sputtered and fractured. Dust and boards rained from the splits, which, staying vigilant, Ruth was careful to avoid. When she saw Nate up ahead, she hit the brakes, skidding through the grime and shards of furniture.

"Nate," she yelled. "Nate!"

He didn't respond but only glared back with apprehension stapled to his stare and an eerie stillness nailed to his bones.

Something was off. Nate was not himself. He looked the same but different. He seemed *off*. His eyes glowed with specs of yellow. His figure had a silver edge to it that shimmered in the light of the half-moon that snuck between the cracks in the brick. Eminence encircled his presence. A clotted swallow hit the back of Ruth's throat. She hesitated to move closer but did so carefully. Balling her hands into knotted fists, she felt the tension surge to her elbows. She kept her head level with his and her eyes level with his own.

"I thought I knew you, but you want the world to ignite, and you don't care if your friends go up with it," she said as she trudged closer, not shifting her gaze from the madness lurking behind his. "Seeing you like this is like recognizing someone I've never met, but I'm not afraid of you."

Nate's body had a heavenly shine to it. He was like some crown diamond under hot museum lights, the direction of light shafts slicing the stone at just the right angles to make it glitter all the more. Finally, words spilled out audibly into the falling room, but Nate's mouth stayed shut. "Yet you tremble as though you are."

"I'm scared for you more than I'm scared of you. Were you trying to kill us, Nate? By bringing us here. Were we in your way?"

"You wanted to come here just as much as I did. Admit it. Admit why you really came here in the first place, why you came back."

"You can read minds, Nate. Do I really need to say it?"

"You need to say it for yourself."

"I've always envied your accomplishments. I know your parents are important people, but you've done well for your age, very well. My family has nothing."

"You thought you could take—"

"I thought I could learn from you. You have gifts. More than I even knew. You wanted me to come, didn't you?"

Nate said nothing.

"Am I a scapegoat? Am I anything to you?" Ruth continued.

"I don't need a scapegoat," he said. "I will not fail. I will not slip. I am unending."

"You don't know what you are. That's why you came here in the first place. Now you think you know, and it terrifies you. And we should never be afraid of who we really are."

Ruth stepped nearer to Nate's shimmering life-force with less reluctance. His devilish, starlit eyes with the two deep pits tucked in between each yellow iris glowed like lava."Who we spend time with reflects who we are underneath. I am a reflection of you," said Nate.

"I guess I am afraid of you then."

"No, you're afraid of what you've become. You thought you wanted power, but you know what you'll do with it. You know control will evade you. You know only I can tame the beast inside. Only I can eat his flesh, while you'll be left to starve on fear."

"There's one difference between us. I don't have to fight to be myself."

"If you don't have to fight to be yourself, then you don't know yourself…"

Nate faded like a spirit, like a vapor in the breeze, but his leer did not. It remained, and those yellow eyes from hell stayed planted in the room, lingering in the air. As Ruth drew nearer to them, she saw something that made her skin crawl. Her lips quivered, her fingers each a dying slug, fidgeting, and her unblinking eyes shot wide as they became the same menacing gold as Nate's were—as sneaky, as slippery. As demonic.

Only just before the first tear fell did she realize that in the exact spot where Nate had been standing was a sliver mirror, long and gleaming with contempt. In the reflection, Nate's yellow eyes were Ruth's, and the ceiling came down with all its might and crushed her.

14

Through the ajar door, Nate scanned the hallway he had created that allowed him and Olivia to evade the clutches of the demon once again. The hall was loaded with identical doors, forty some in all. Nate's temples protruded from his skull as thirty more matching doors grew onto the walls.

Nate retreated back into the room, which was nothing more than a basic bedroom, or so it appeared. The mahogany double bed at the far end of the room had four posts around its finely carved frame. There was a dresser and a window next to it that pulled in a sliver of the moon to provide some visibility in the otherwise pitch blackness.

Nate dragged Olivia and slung her behind the bed, where they hid in the security of the headboard. In their brief second of hiding while the demon scoured the other doors, Nate pondered the rules of the mind game they were playing. He believed that if he had the mental capacity to alter the house's architecture, why could he not move himself and Olivia as well? His plan was to jump them from room to room until daylight arrived or the demon wore thin. He wasn't sure if it would work, but he was too spent to think of anything wiser.

CLICK, CLICK, CLACK, CLICK, CLICK, CLACK snuck under the bedroom door and tapped on Nate and Olivia's eardrums. It was a pestering sound meant to crack Nate's focus: the sound of talons haunting the wood in an impatient patter and claws tempting the plaster. That awful, shadowed beast was checking the rooms one by one. After it had done so, a swooshing noise swept in dust from the hall. What was it? More clacking and swooshing followed.

Why was the demon so persistent? Hadn't they determined that Nate was weak and lacked the ability to achieve anything of significance? Hadn't they decided that Nate was indeed too afraid to be himself and accept himself? Why then did it care? What did it want with him? Was it going to kill him for the sheer joy of it? As the swooshing came closer to their door, Nate understood what it was. It was the sound of each room disappearing. The demon was checking the room and then eliminating it from existence.

Then, right outside the door, a foul stench crept into the room. The smell was repulsive and perverted, and it wrestled away any remaining breathable air that the mold painted on the walls had left. It was the kind of reek that flustered the nostrils, the smell of a thousand unflushed toilets brimming with excrement, and beside the toilets were a thousand decaying bodies adorned with charred flesh. It was the odor of chaos, of lunacy, of destruction. It was paralyzing, and their ruptured eyes abounded with tears against its potency.

Pressed together behind the back of the headboard, Nate wrapped Olivia into his body, shielding her from what was to come. He laced his fingers in her dark brown curls. The wads felt like silk on his fingertips. The smoothness of the strands was calming, and though death was knocking at the door and Nate was at the brink of exhaustion, for the first time in his entire life, peace soared in his veins and pumped in his gut. At that instance, Nate understood he had never really known—let alone held in his own two arms—someone who cared so dearly for him, someone who was willing to sit with him on the cliff of annihilation and go over it if she had to. The feeling was sweet and enriching, as if his soul was singing. Somehow, buried in this girl who barely comprehended the notion of faith, was something beyond love incarnate.

Jump, he thought, *jump! If not for me, for her. I must save her. I must protect this last grape of chastity dangling on the vine of guilt.* Surging his muscles, he fought for the thought of a different room. His brain bulged, his jaw stretched, and his toes warped inward. *Another room*, he thought, *another room. Any room! Anywhere but here!*

Then the thought of recognition struck him like a club. He knew this room. It was *his* room, with his father's old hunting rifle leaning in the corner, his Bible open to Proverbs on the dresser, and the milkshake fountain glass he'd saved from the dinner before the Road Rabbits game. He also had the foul ball his father caught and gave to him, but the glass meant more. It meant his father remembered, and Nate would never forget. In this same place where his view of his father was broken and reconstructed and broken, where he would speak to God, where his relationship with his Lord was built, he would now face the demon that threatened to extinguish who he had become.

Nate could not outthink the demon. He had not one ounce of strength left. This is why the demon manipulated him and kept him in that dreadful room all day. It was the degradation of his senses. It was the preparation for possession. He knew the demon could go a thousand more rounds, and he couldn't. The demon was some unceasing being, some entity that pulled from a pool of dark yet unlimited energy. "The mad never grow sad," his father used to say.

Suddenly, the height of the room rose, and the bed disintegrated. The mahogany melted to a puddle of shards. Submission was the truth. Submission was the reality. *I must submit*, he thought. *I don't want to, but I don't care to fight anymore. I can't fight anymore. Therefore, I must submit.*

Bars strapped a square cross on the window—the same as the window in the attic. From its elevated position, the moon's rays hit the demon from the front and the side. The demon's horned and sadistic shape morphed with the cross shadow from the bars. Punctured by the ridges in the demon's skin, the cross appeared deformed and mutilated. It was one with the shadow of the demon.

Nate turned toward the diabolical figure and forced himself to behold its towering presence. It was a breathing nightmare. Phantasmal, it stood over ten feet tall. Moonlight caught in the yellow of the demon's eyes and made them sparkle like knives. The eyes didn't frighten Nate like they did before. Now, they enticed him. There was a majesty in their crooked nature. Hate could be artful, he supposed. Death could be graceful.

The wall behind Nate and Olivia vanished. A pit replaced it and stretched down some thirty floors. At the bottom was a faint light to show the nature of its end. Shards of glass and spikes of metal speared upward. It was a bed of blades, and it would pulverize any who was drawn to its jagged fist.

"Do you not see, Nathan? Do you not see the truth? You never left the room. You never left *the dark*. You will never leave it," snarled the demon.

The shimmering ruby juice was a glossy ocean in the wine glass, with its breakers ready to kiss and devour. Amir studied the glass in his clenched hand, hypnotized by its decadent contents. The syrup sang to him. Under his nose, the scent was blissful and garden-esque. Amir brought the lid to his mouth with careful consideration. The blood of the cherries grazed his lips. The sweet, maiden nectar dribbled down his chin. Amir drank and drank and drank. When he turned to return the now-empty glass to the man, he was met with a sheet of thick limestone coated in overgrowth. It was the exterior wall of the house. Somehow, he'd arrived there. He had not known they were this close. Looking back over his shoulder, toward the officers, he saw their flashlights were trained on him, beaming in his face.

"We fou-foun-found it," said Amir with uncertainty. His tongue was heavy and slow. The words tumbled and slurred. "I kn-I know the way in-in-inside."

One of the flashlights caught the glass in Amir's hand.

"What's he got there?" someone yelled.

"He's tryin' to pull a fast one, chief," said another.

"Easy boys, let's see what he's got," the sheriff warned.

"It-it-it's right there-right here," fumbled Amir.

"Ah, he's been drinking. I don't like this. It's the same as the last time. He's tryin' to pull somethin', chief. Why else would he bring us way out here?"

"Amir, put it down. This ain't no boy who cried wolf, but it's darn near close. You've been ropin' us along for too long, son. Now, drop it," said the sheriff, and a winding clack finished off his words. His gun was ready to fire.

"Right here," Amir motioned to the house, raising up the glass, which was only a sliver of shine to the police. Pistols rose and aimed at Amir, and the hammers slammed back. As the police opened fire and riddled his body with bullets, the shots flew through the stone wall like cannon fire. As Amir was blasted to bits, the house blasted right back at the police, spraying them with ivy-wrapped debris. Before they could swivel to evade, the stone tumbled and flattened each of them. The house continued to tilt and wobble, its splitting clamor piercing over the deafening buzz of the cicadas. Dust-covered streams of blood tiptoed between the bits of rubble and rolled out into the tired night.

"Jus' a taste," said the wrinkled man—that devious Unraveler—as he moved around the bed toward the EKG monitor and IV stand. His shadow hung heavy on the wall and glided like a devil. On the silver table beside the bed, a small glass vial sat delicately on the cold metal. The vial read: MORPHINE.

"Nurse mus' a not notice that makeup when she was runnin' yer IV. Otherwise, she'd surely not a left this here. She'd a known about your little issue and a known ya couldn't resist."

Daphne scratched, screamed for words, but her throat was parched, and her tongue stuck to the roof of her mouth.

"Yer friends deserted ya as if you was roadkill. They ain't comin' back. They gon' keep drivin' on down that dusty highway without as much as a glance in the rearview."

The bed sheets twisted and balled inside Daphne's grip, which kept reeling them toward her. Her neck slanted and curled, as she dove for the strength to lift her wearied head off the pillow. When the words came, they came with a false confidence and flawed assuredness. When they came, they were raspy and broken. They came with all she had left—

"They're... coming... back."

He tapped his skin-rolled hooks on the bed frame and had a little whistle in his breath before he said, "I do applaud yer fortatude, but they ain't comin' back cause ya ain't got no friends to begin with."

"Liar... Your lies are so blatant... even an addict on the edge of a rush can spot them. Words hold no weight, and you're nothing more than words." Daphne's lips quivered with the statement, as if she didn't believe what she was saying but desperately wanted to.

"Face the validitness of what I say, they don' care about you. Never did."

"They do," said Daphne. Her tears were a flooding river eroding her cheeks.

"Even yer *friend*, Nate. The one ya went all that way for. He hardly know ya exist."

"He's the one who invited me."

"Cause he knew what'd happen to ya. He want to get rid of ya. And Ruth, she pay to get rid of ya.

Nobody, even somebody they love, don' wanna be stalked aroun' like that. That's you. Always hangin' 'bout. Face what I say, only friend ya ever had was a needle."

Daphne's eyes snapped away from the Unraveler to the open of the cold room. They studied its emptiness, then drifted.

"World's as cold as this place," said the Unraveler. "Even the doctors forget 'bout you. But don' you worry. I haven't." He placed a quiet hand over his heart and closed his eyes and bowed slightly. "I know, 'lieve me, I know. Takin' care of yer friends is one hell of a burden, 'specially ones that don' care to remember yer there. You was the one that went after 'im. I know you was the one. Listen here, no one'll blame ya."

"I'm so sick of being alone, even when I'm with them."

"I got the cure. Right 'ere."

The needle slid into the vial with ease, and as his decrepit hands arched back the bow of the syringe, a red, pulpy liquid pumped inside it. The needle was wide, and in its chrome reflection, a pair of yellow, corrupted eyes met Daphne's. They were her eyes.

"Want me to, or would ya like the honor?"

In submission, Daphne shut her eyes with finality and peace and lay back on the cushiony bed. She released her hold on the sheets and let them furl back into place. Her breath steadied, and the tension in her body calmed like the sea after a storm. The waves rocked with care.

"Goes down easy," he said, and he released the red arrow of death into her IV line. The ceiling bulbs shrieked and blasted bright. The paint on the walls chipped as they trembled and heaved. The room shook violently. The sea raged back into a storm, and what was left of Daphne's ship sank below the waves as the EKG ran flat.

Backing to the edge of the cliff with the deadly crags below, Nate positioned Olivia behind him to guard her from the claw that was rising up as though it were the mighty hand of God. Those wicked, pattering talons teased on the hollow boards from which the gnarled and knotted creature grew taller with each grotesque step. Its features etched sharper from its tortured form like writhing snakes.

"What do you say, Nathan? Have you discovered purpose in the void? Have you found your calling in the emptiness?" said the demon.

"I've discovered death is all I deserve. Kill me if it's what you came to do," said Nate.

"Nate, look at me," said Olivia, as her hand turned his face to her with a soft gentleness. "This isn't you. This isn't who you were called to be," she said.

"I wasn't called to be anything. If God called me, he wouldn't have left me."

"Maybe He has left you, Nate, but didn't you leave, also?"

"An eye for an eye," said Nate with a sick grin smeared on his lips. Olivia's calm became stark and stern as she saw his eyes become as shiny and yellow as the Sun, and they burned just as hot. Submerged in the twilight amber, his pupils were deep and soul-shattering. They gave him an aura so evil that the rot on the walls receded for shelter.

Fighting the fear in her cheeks, she let her tight muscles slacken and cradled Nate's cheek with a tender palm, stroking it with her whispering thumb.

"We are all the same, Olivia," said the demon, but the words came from Nate's mouth. "We are all God, and we are all nothing."

"You're only nothing in the dark, where you can't see what you are, but even there, He sees you," said Olivia. "Even there, I see you."

"I do not want to kill you, Nathan," said the demon from his own thin and pointed lips that began to curl upward at the edges into a diabolical grin. "I never wanted that. However, even should you resist me, your fate is sealed. It is impossible for those who have seen the light and shared in the gift of God and who have fallen away to return to the faith. You see it now, do you not? You see why you are necessary."

"Yes," said Nate, "I see why I'm necessary, but what I don't see… is why you are."

Nate lunged at the demon and jolted it backward. Now, beneath the clawed creature was the same pit, the same trap the demon had laid for him, and they were plunging toward it with unstoppable force. Nate was renewed with a strength he had never known.

His eyes were desert gold and formidable. Sin crested in them, yes, but there was also vigor and bravery. As they plummeted toward their hideous end, entangled in a spinning twine, Nate understood why the demon was, in fact, necessary. For his final thought, he imagined the exit for Olivia.

Olivia peered over the drop and saw them tumbling toward the beastly shards until finally both the demon and Nate were impaled on them, their bodies mangled and sprawled like rag dolls. Olivia's emotions bubbled up to her welling eyes and labored breaths. Overwhelmed with relief and grief, she turned to see a door behind her leading out to the hallway with the original velvet and elm staircase that descended back to the main floor. She peered out into the hall. All was steady. The walls bore wounds of splintering fissures. A web of fractures dressed the floorboards, which rose and bent in lumps. But despite the wreckage, all was respite.

Making it down the staircase, through the kitchen and the library and the room with tall windows, she saw that each had slightly more debris than before, but overall, maintained shape. Soon, she was back on the veranda and out of that great and terrible place. Gazing out from the high, long deck, the sun was rising in the distance, and the dawn forged into existence an almighty air that was valiant and enduring. The crisp rays of sunlight cut into shade and wove through the stone balusters on the balcony railing in smooth slats.

Olivia absorbed it for a moment. The day was already getting hot, even though it had barely begun. The sparrows and the chickadees were chirping and excited for the light, excited at the possibilities of what the light brought. The sea of weeds and oaks and cypresses resting below the horizon were a reminder that day must come, and it always does. The honeysuckle, mixed with coneflower, mixed with milkweed, was the scent of the sunrise. The world was alive, and it was green and beautiful.

Olivia scaled down the rear wall of the home and circled back toward the front. From the outside, the damage was minuscule, and the cracks were mostly obscured. It did not appear to be a structure that just moments ago was on the verge of collapse. The sheets of pollen on the statues and the limestone had vanished, as if a sharp wind had swept in and dusted them clean. Marbled gleamed in the light of the hopeful day.

The even humidity was fresh and renewing in Olivia's lungs and tasted rich. She stood before the vine-covered castle, soaking in its sheer size and greatness. The sun appeared as an angel's halo as it climbed over the back of the house, and its powerful rays curved around the ornate chimneys and gargoyles and dormers.

Though Olivia's expression clutched at disdain, somewhere in those clenched lips sat admiration for the beast, perhaps even curiosity. The fountain was still, and the curled marble smiled at the daylight. She ran her hand over the curves once again, intrigued by the absence of their decay. The day was at peace, and it was ready to begin.

Olivia turned and headed back down the drive toward the gate when she heard something rather odd. Behind her, she heard something that shot a tear down her eye so fast you could miss it. She was frozen but somehow managed to walk forward anyway, though it was slow and laborious. Behind her were footsteps. But these were not human feet. They were heavy and ungodly. The tears fell harder, but her feet couldn't move faster. The steps behind her weren't chasing her, but they were following her, and they were sinister.

Olivia kept her pace, though it was grueling. The weight of an eternal pressure, like being deep under water, was contorting her features. The footsteps were heavier and closer. Olivia let out an audible yelp. She couldn't hide the fear that was swallowing her. CLOSER the feet stepped, which seemed to have a pattering motion, where the toes clattered on the gravel. Olivia couldn't bring herself to turn around. She kept going for the gate, which looked jagged and sickly. Its iron spired and twisted into the sky. Its height was more menacing than it appeared when they had arrived, but it was the only safety Olivia could find.

She began to run, kicking up gravel in bunches. Tears streamed from her terrified eyes that squinted through the cracks in her glasses. The footsteps ran with her. They were gaining. They were *CLOSER*. They were angry.

Olivia slipped between the opening of the gate and slammed the iron bars shut with a clang. She pushed them together with all her might, clenching the rods in her palms and then carefully backing away, trembling. Her mouth opened wide but could hardly catch breath. The tears continued. Her face contorted, and her body twitched. She was looking up at something between the bars, waiting behind the iron. The footsteps were no more, and the gate did not open after her, but still, something captivated her focus. She could not steel herself from that which was before her. And in the reflection of her weathered lenses was something round, something yellow, something evil. The reflection did not blink. It did not waver. It did not show any emotion but knowing and hate.

AROUND – The Game

You've read the book, now it's time to step into the shoes of the characters. Play AROUND - The Game—an immersive and terrifying, first-person experience inside the world of the novel. You can download and play the game on the App Store, Android, or PC by going to https://www.aroundthen ovel.com/game or by scanning the QR code below with your smartphone or tablet.